SPELLHORN

Berlie Doherty was born in Knotty Ash, Liverpool, the youngest of three children. She always wanted to be a writer, but when she was little there were many things she wanted to be – a singer, ballet dancer, air hostess, librarian... Her serious writing started at university, where she trained to be a teacher. She has won the Carnegie Medal twice, for *Dear Nobody* and *Granny Was A Buffer Girl*. Now she lives in an isolated cottage in the country and writes in a barn overlooking the Pennines. She says of her writing: "After I finish a book I'm quite sad because I feel grieved that I have lost someone close; a great deal of myself is in my books."

Spellhorn

by

Berlie Doherty

Illustrated by John Lupton

An imprint of HarperCollinsPublishers

First published in Great Britain by Hamish Hamilton Ltd 1989
First published by Collins 1990
First published as a Collins Modern Classic 2002

1 3 5 7 9 8 6 4 2

Collins is an imprint of HarperCollins*Publishers* Ltd, 77–85 Fulham Palace Road,
Hammersmith, London W6 8JB

The HarperCollins website address is www.**fire**and**water**.com

ISBN 0 00 712406 6

Printed and bound in England by Clays Ltd, St Ives plc

For Holly DeArden, Richard Gaynor, David Hathaway and Robert Starling of Tapton Mount School for the Visually Impaired in Sheffield, who helped me to see with my mind's eye.

With special thanks to their teacher, Pat Darley, who gave me a great deal of help and encouragement; and also to Janet Whitaker of BBC Radio 4, who first made me think about unicorns.

CONTENTS

Chapter One

THE WATCHER ON THE HILL

NIGHT IS FALLING. Far down in the valley warm house lights begin to glow. People come home from work and close their doors behind them.

To the watcher on the hill the scene is strange. He has never seen a modern village before. The moving cars with their searching sweep of lights alarm him. He can just hear the low drone of their voices. Yet there is something comforting, too, in the sight of the glow of lights strung together across the darkness. He is fascinated by the boy on the wheeled beast, prowling silently up and down, up and down, the main street. The eye of the beast is pale and faltering. The watcher sees no danger there.

His rough-haired horse is impatient. He stamps the ground restlessly and tosses his head round, anxious to be back with his fellows. His rider lays a restraining hand on his neck. Away behind him he can hear the crackling and spurting that tells him that the Wild Ones have lit their fires for the night. There will be food for him after his long day's searching. Yet he hasn't done what he's set out to do. There'll be anger and grief, and a time of terrible revenge, he knows that.

He kicks his horse's haunches with his bare heels, turning as the horse wheels round, and takes one last look at the village settling itself for sleep. He can't explain the feeling of deep sadness that comes over him then.

"Well, Froth. My eyes are full of all this now. Back home!"

The boy on the bike was Sam. It was his birthday, and the bike was a present from his parents. It was second-hand, but his mum had painted it up for him. He wasn't sure he liked the saddle. He'd have to lower it, and maybe he'd change the handle-bar grips, and then he'd ride round and show it off to his friends. Tim and Ian would want to ride it, of course, but he wouldn't let them. They'd have the wheels buckled in no time, charging into pot-holes. But Laura, his best friend, would want to touch it. He knew that she would crouch down and run her hands over the cold steel of its frame, learning the shape of it. She'd press the rubber tyres gently, noticing the pattern on the rim, and she'd run the backs of her fingers over the spokes as if they were a musical instrument, making them chime with her nails. He'd let her sit on it if she wanted to, and he'd push her along for a bit, up and down the pavements round her house. She'd love that. Maybe he'd fit her feet into the toe-clips and let her listen to the wheels whirring as she pedalled. But he'd never let go.

"Sam!" his mum called, as he practised a skid-stop. "Come on in now."

"In a bit, Mum."

"Now. Those lights aren't strong enough for night-riding. I've told you that. And it's cold."

"Boiling."

"And have you seen what time it is? Come on, Sam."

With a sigh that admitted defeat Sam rammed his pedals down and skidded to a halt by the milk bottles.

Laura's house was at the end of the valley. She stood by the open window of her bedroom, enjoying the cold touch of the night wind on her face and the swish of the curtains against her arms. Night always had a cold sharp smell. The wind had tangled up the flowers in her garden, and she could just catch their faint, familiar perfume. She was about to move away when she caught a new scent. She leaned out of her window again, trying to breathe it in. It was rich and deep and spicy. In her mind she called it damask.

"It's cold in here, Laura." Her mother came up behind her and touched her arm as she spoke. "Close the window now."

"My garden smells lovely tonight."

"Does it? Must be that new fertiliser your dad put down."

Laura could hear the amusement in her mother's voice as she drew the curtains to, crinkling the hooks on their runner.

The rider could hear the shouting and laughter of his people as he drew near to them. He could recognise the deep, growly singing of his old father, Sideman, and the lighter voice of his son, Sloe. The women were talking quietly round their own small fire. Their work for the day was done now; they wouldn't move till morning. The men heard him coming and shouted noisily to him to join them. He was so hungry that he could have eaten where he was, on Froth's back. But he had a job to do first.

"Where's the Old Woman?" he asked Sloe, as the boy came running to him with a horn of warm wine. Sloe nodded towards the smaller fires, and as if she'd heard her name through all that shouting and clamour she stood up, flicking her long white hair back over her shoulders.

"Well, Wayfinder," she shouted, and her wavering voice drove all the singing away. "Have you found him for me?"

He shook his head.

"Well?" she shouted again, her blank face turned like a moon towards him.

"No, Old Woman. Not yet. But I have sense in my mind-hole that he's somewhere round about."

"Then why for does he stay away from me?" All that could be seen of her in the darkness was the pale cloak of her hair as she moved from fire to fire, stepping and stumbling over the sprawling figures. Sloe ran to help her. When she reached Wayfinder she put her hand out to stroke Froth's back. Then she turned round to the Wild Ones, her head thrust forward, her eyes peering.

The old man, Sideman, came over to stand by her. He put up both his hands.

"Wild Ones, stop sounds!" he shouted. "The Old Woman has wordsayings for you."

The Wild Ones muttered as the Old Woman spoke to them.

"What's happening to us?" she asked. "We've wandered here far from our Wilderness. He brought us here and now he's left us. What is he searching for, Wild Ones, do you know? We'll die here in our last forever sleep if we stay. This is no country for Wild Ones, this land."

They grunted in agreement.

"And step by step my eyes are growing dimmer. I have no sight of your faces, only the flickerings of your fires. I can see the moon-eye in the sky, but I can't see her shadowings on earth. Night is nuzzling round me. And I think in my mind-hole I know why. Do you? Do you?"

"We know why, Old Woman," grunted Sideman.

"It's because my unicorn has gone. My eyebright turns to darkness without him, he knows that. And yet he leaves me here. Where's my Spellhorn, Sideman?"

He put his hands over his eyes and shook his head. "We followed our noses far in the night, sniffing for him…"

"He had no why for to go away from us. Where is he?"

"Perhaps he's been snatched," Sloe suggested.

The Old Woman laughed bitterly. "Snatched, is it? Is that what you think in your mind-hole? Your father's given you no wordsense at all. Keep this in your rememberings for ever, Sloe. Unicorns aren't snatched! No time! Not while there's life breath in them, that's for sure."

Cold silence fell on the Wild Ones then, like the hush of snow. They turned uneasily away from their fires, watching the Old Woman, their leader. Every one of them had the same thought in their heads, but only Sloe was rash enough to say it.

"Then if he hasn't been snatched, he must have taken the long forever sleep."

The Old Woman shuddered. "If he's in last sleep, then I'm for last sleep, too. And all of you, know that. There's no wayback to the Wilderness, not without Spellhorn. The Wild Ones are waylost for ever."

The watchers round the fires kept their silence. Sideman, the Old Woman's closest friend, clucked deep in the back of his throat. He threaded his twisted fingers through the long strands of his beard. "We can't stay here," he said. "This is no life place for Wild Ones."

"I've been to eye spy round the manfolk shelters," said Wayfinder. "Over in the dipdown there, Old Woman. And I had noseful of him then. I don't believe he's snatched or dead."

"Then what?" The Old Woman turned her sightless face up to his. "Why has he left us, waylost and heartsad?"

Wayfinder slid off Froth's back, allowing the horse to trot over to its brothers. He was trying to think what to tell the Old Woman without causing her more hurt. "Perhaps he has heartlongings to stay down there."

The Old Woman brought her hands to her face and pressed her cheekbones back. In the dance of firelight you could see her skull under her flesh; hollows in skin, black deeps of eyes. Now there was no sound to hear except the shifting of logs in the fires, and the snorting of the horses at their feeding.

"Find Spellhorn!" She swung away from Sloe and Wayfinder and walked slowly back to the women's fire. The Wild Ones moved to let her pass, and no one helped her over the uneven ground. Sloe turned to his father anxiously.

"But how can we find him – if he's in last sleep, or if he's been snatched, or if he's run away from us – we have no heart-hope to find him now."

The Old Woman had stopped at her sleeping-place. She leaned forward into the flames of her fire so that their light danced bright on her face and her arms. Strands of white hair fell forward, curling to singe. Her eyes gleamed with the fire's gold.

"Flame him out!" she said. "Take fire to the shelters of the dipdown, and watch him creep out for air. He can't live in firesmoke. Flame him out, burn them down! But bring my Spellhorn back safekeep to me."

Chapter Two

NIGHT OF FIRE

LAURA WOKE TO the sound of hooves pounding down the hillside. It was so loud it seemed to strike the rock deep beneath the earth. She could hear the shouting of men's voices, urging the horses on, and mingled with their cries she could hear the faint crackling of flames.

"Mum!" she shouted. "Mum! Quick! What's happening?"

Her mother called back from her own room and then came in to her.

"What's up with you, Laura?" she grumbled. "You woke me up." As she put the light on she saw that Laura was sitting up stiffly in bed, her face white with terror. She came to her and put her arms round her. "Laura? What's the matter?"

"Where are the horses going?" Laura asked.

"Horses?" Her mother was puzzled. "What d'you mean, horses?"

"There's wild horses, and men with loud voices, and flames!"

"I don't know what you're talking about." Her mother, cross again at being woken up for nothing, stood up to go back to bed. "You've dreamt it, love. There's no horses."

"I can hear them," Laura insisted. "They're going down into the valley. And the men are shouting and laughing…"

To please her, Laura's mother went over to the window and drew the curtains. She pushed open the window and leaned out. The night was still and calm. The wind of early evening had dropped; nothing moved.

Laura covered her ears to block out the terrible sound of the beating hooves.

"You must stop this," her mother said firmly. "There's no horses. Off you go, back to sleep."

She tucked Laura up and went out. But she left the

light on and the door open so she could watch her daughter. And Laura lay with her eyes wide open, listening to the danger in the valley. She could hear the restless neighing of the horses far away, and the wild yelling and laughter. And then she heard the crackling of fire. She could smell it now, sharp and acrid. The houses in the main street had been set alight. Sam's house would be on fire. She sat up in bed again, willing him to think of her so she could warn him.

"Sam!" she shouted. "Sam!"

Sam didn't know what had woken him up. As soon as he sat up in bed he could smell smoke. He ran to his bedroom door, opened it, and to his horror saw smoke curling up from the downstairs rooms. It stung his eyes like needles. He ran across the landing to his parents' room and pushed their door open.

"Fire!" he shouted. "The house is on fire!"

Before his parents could get out of bed even, he'd edged his way carefully through the smoke downstairs and out into the street. Smoke was pouring from the doors and windows of his neighbours' houses. He ran up and down the street, banging on doors and shouting, "Fire! Fire!" and soon he was joined by his parents. In no time the street was in chaos as people rushed out in their night clothes, swinging buckets of water on the flames, coughing and choking and pulling each other back from the sour smoke. Fire engines arrived and men ran with long snaking hoses, trying to train them on as many buildings as they could. Sam remembered his bike and rushed round the side of the house for it.

"Sam! Where are you going?" his mother screamed.

"I want to get my bike!" he shouted.

His father tried to pull him back but he'd already swung open the door of the garage and was wheeling his bike out.

"You little fool!" his father shouted at him. "There's a car full of petrol in there! If that had gone up you'd have gone with it!"

Guttering fell from the roofs, long spars with leaping flames, and people screamed as they ran back away from them. Gusts of wind blew charred smoke in great billows. The dying flames sizzled as the water hoses took hold, and the air was bitter with the smell of burnt wood.

But at last the fires were all extinguished. Sam and his neighbours stood huddled in the grey light of early morning; their homes gone.

The Old Woman waited impatiently for the Wild Ones' return. She could smell the smoke in the valley, and hear the clamour, and she heard the horses return and the men talking excitedly to each other. It took her some time to

find Wayfinder. He and Sloe were standing together on
the brink of the hill, looking down in silence at the glow
of flames in the valley. Their horses, Fen and Froth,
tugged at the grasses, unwilling to move away from their
masters when they were in this strange mood.

"Well?" she asked them, clinging on to Sloe's arm to
steady herself. "Have you found him?"

"Not yet time," Wayfinder said. The skin of his fingers
was scorched where he'd burnt them on the torch of
flame. He wanted to plunge his hands into a stream to
relieve his pain, but the Old Woman stopped him as he
turned away.

"But no eyesight of him?"

"No, Old Woman. I have heart-hope that he's down
there, even now, in some hiding-hole."

"We flamed some shelters," Sloe told her.

"How many?"

"A handful," Wayfinder said. "And half my fingers. I
want to get them made well. Is Healhands here?"

She dodged in front of him again. "And why have you
stopped? My Mighty High words were to flame him till
you'd smoked him out!"

Wayfinder looked at Sloe over her head. How could
he describe the terror of the Wild Ones when the alarm
had been sent up and the fire engines had come blaring
their sirens down the streets?

"Give her word-pictures of the monsters, Sloe," he said, and walked away. His own thoughts were with the men and women and children who had run in terror from their smoking homes. Wayfinder had been told when he was a boy that he would never make a fighter, he was too gentle. Childheart, his mother sometimes called him.

"Red monsters came for us," Sloe told the Old Woman. "They were huge beasts with flashing eyes and snake heads, and they ate the flames with water. We were skinshaken in fright."

A frail and skinny young Wild Woman danced round him and laughed.

"Skinshaken!"

"Right sure!" Sloe protested. "We had heart fear, all of us."

"Poor Sloe!" she laughed again. "Did you take earful of that, Water! Heart fear! Only worms have heart fear!"

"Be tongue-still, Flight!" Water scolded her.

Flight glanced round at the other Wild Women with her bright bird eyes. "It's my thinking that the girls and women should do the search around now. Why leave it to the Wildmen when they have worm hearts?"

Water clucked at Flight. "It's the boy's first dashdown with the Wildmen. Give him chance!"

Flight sidled up to Sloe like a cat, pouting at him.

"Sloe, let me do the dashdown too. I know the unicorn will come to me…"

"No time!" the Old Woman snapped. Flight pulled her lips back over her teeth at her, knowing the Old Woman couldn't see her.

"I'm the Mighty High," the Old Woman reminded her. "And Spellhorn is all mine. Hold that forever in your mind-hole."

"Then you find him, Old Bones!" Flight muttered.

Sideman caught her arm and gripped it till it hurt. "I'll hurl you in nettles, with your tongue of snakes!" he told her.

"I'm thinking Spellhorn's left us all for good," Sloe said in a small voice. He had his back to them all. He could still see the gusts of yellow smoke in the valley.

"Never no time say that," the Old Woman moaned. "My Mighty High's all gone without my unicorn. Seek him, all of you! Smoke him out of his hiding-holes. You must!"

Wayfinder and Sloe watched her as she shuffled away with the Wild Women. For the first time in his life Sloe knew that he wasn't afraid of her.

"Did you catch smell of him, Sloe?" Wayfinder asked.

The boy nodded.

"Deep in my nose, and here and there like sweetsmoke in the hill. But I didn't catch glimpse of him."

"Neither did I. But why is he shadowing in manfolk shelters? Puzzlement," said Wayfinder. "Great strange puzzlement."

Laura's father had been driving through the village when the fire started. He stayed down there to help as much as he could, and had ended up driving Sam's mother and father to the hospital for treatment for shock, and bringing Sam back to stay with them for a week or two. He was put straight to bed in the spare room and when Laura got up the next day he was still asleep.

While she was waiting for him to get up she went out to do some work in her little garden. The weak October sun warmed her as she worked. Her mother had given her some bulbs for spring, and she wanted to get them planted before winter frosts set in. She carried a small mat out and placed it on the grass, then went back into the shed for her basket of hand tools and the bag of bulbs. She bumped into something bulky and unsteady, and she put her basket down and gently ran her hands over it. It was cold and smooth, a hollowed skeleton frame, with rubber wheels. She steadied it back against the shed side and took her basket out.

Yesterday she'd prepared the soil by turning it over and by digging a narrow trench to set the bulbs in. She knelt down on her mat and leaned forward to bury the bulbs in the earth. She knew the hairy bits went in first and that the spiky top would soon nose up through the soil and towards the light. She placed the first bulb in, and firmed the moist earth round it, trickling it through her fingers and pressing it down with the palm of her hands. A soft worm slithered across. She would plant the second bulb two hand-widths away from the first.

She measured the distance and then paused, stroking the earth gently with her fingers. It was different. The soil was dented. Something had been there in the night. She felt along the trench until she found another dent, and then leaned forward to find two more. Four strange dents. She knelt back, wondering, puzzled. A strange, rich scent wafted round her. She breathed it in deeply. Now, as faint as wind stirring autumn leaves, she heard a restless shuffling of hooves.

"Hello, Laura."

Laura looked round, as startled as if she'd suddenly been woken up from a sleep.

"Sam!" she said. "You frightened the life out of me."

"Didn't you hear me coming?" he asked, concerned. "I made a lot of noise on the path, on purpose."

"I was miles away," she said. She felt awkward suddenly, remembering what had happened in the night. "Are you all right?"

"Oh, yes. I'm all right. Move over." He squatted down on the mat next to her. "It was horrible, though."

"What about your mum and dad?"

"They're OK. Your mum just rang the hospital for me. They're going to go and stay at my gran's. We won't be able to go back home for ages."

"That's awful," Laura said. "I'd hate to lose my home. Especially my bedroom. All my special things. Did everything get burnt?"

"Most things. I managed to save my bike. It's in your shed now."

"I know. I nearly fell over it."

They both laughed. Laura picked another bulb from her basket and rolled it lightly from one hand to the other. Its loose, papery skin crackled.

"Sam. Did you hear the horses?"

"Horses? When?"

"Last night."

"There weren't any horses. I thought I heard someone shouting my name, though. It woke me up."

"That was me," said Laura. "I did our game, where we try to make each other think the same things. I knew your house was on fire."

They were both silent, considering this. Laura's house was a mile away from Sam's, and halfway up the hillside. He couldn't possibly have heard her.

Sam shook his head. "And then I smelt burning and I ran out to tell people. I couldn't believe it when I saw all those other houses on fire, as well. I think if I hadn't woken up so soon we'd have had some terrible accidents. People would have been burnt. Killed."

His voice shook. He picked at a spike of straw sticking out from Laura's basket. "Who could have done a thing like that?"

"The horse-riders did it," Laura said quietly. "I heard them."

Sam stared at her as she leaned forward and patted her hand along the earth trench. "And they came through our garden. Look."

He couldn't make anything of the dents she pointed out to him.

"I can't tell what they are," he said. "Just little hollows. You probably did that when you were digging."

"I know I didn't," Laura told him. "I smoothed it all down. Try and see them, Sam. Close your eyes."

This was the strange game that Laura and Sam had invented for themselves. Sometimes he would describe something that he could see, the colours and the details and all the shinings and shadows of it, till she said she could see it, too. And sometimes she would show him something that she could see in her head. They called it her mind's eye. Sam would close his eyes for a long time, letting his mind focus on the dark blood-red and the blue and golden dance of light-spots and the deep velvet blackness that he could only see behind his eyes. Then Laura would tell him what she could see, and sometimes the sound of her voice would make colours come and go, like shattered pieces of mirror-glass.

Now, as she knelt beside him on the rough kitchen mat, she felt across for his hand and stretched it out. She steadied herself with one palm flat and guided his fingers to the first hollow in the soil.

"Now!" she whispered. "What's been there?"

He patted the soil, feeling round the bumps and hollows of it without opening his eyes. "There could have been something standing here…" he said at last, a little doubtfully.

"Something heavy and leaning," Laura told him. "You can tell where it's pushed into the earth and kind of scuffed it back…"

"Yes," he said slowly. "You can…"

"And here. And here. And here." Laura guided his hand to the other dents. Now he could feel the restless pressure of a heavy creature stamping in the soil. He could almost see it, high-stepping over Laura's trenches. Cold prickles of sweat tickled his hair.

"Can you see it?" Laura whispered.

Sam drew his hand away and opened his eyes, scared.

"Something," he said. "But they're not horse hooves. It's something as big as a horse, but not a horse."

"I know," said Laura quietly. "And it's here now. I know it is."

Chapter Three

THE SOUND OF HORSES

THE MOON THAT night was like water, draining down into a misty sky. The Old Woman lay curled up by her fire, fast asleep. Sideman, her old friend, came to sit by her and waited for her to wake up naturally. He had known very old people to die if they were startled from their sleep. He put a log on the fire. The damp wood spat.

She stirred. "Sideman, is it?"

"You sleep like a moth," he chuckled. "Flutterfingers, twitchlids."

"Listening, that's why," she muttered. She rubbed her dry hands together. "Night frost is down."

"Right sure," he said. "And the moon's big eye is open."

"So what's Wayfinder doing?"

"Waiting for your word-go," Sideman told her. "What's he to do, Old Woman?"

"Same as came last night, same as come tomorrow, till my unicorn comes creeping out of his hiding-hole. I told!"

Sideman raised his hand to Sloe, who in turn signalled Wayfinder, lined up with the other men on their shaggy horses. One by one they trotted past the biggest fire, pausing to dip their wooden torches into the heat of the flames. Sparks spat on to their skins. They lined up, then, in a long row with their flaring torches held high into the dark sky. The horses tugged their heads down to pull at the long grass, and their riders jerked their heads back up again.

The house lights at the near end of the valley gleamed. Some had already been put out for the night. Wayfinder looked across at Sloe.

"Fit for the dashdown?"

Sloe nodded. A thrill of excitement buzzed in his head and tingled like rivers in his arms. He wasn't used to riding with the Wildmen.

Wayfinder raised his arm. "Then away!"

With loud laughter the men kicked their horses on.

Laura woke up to hear them thundering past. She climbed out of bed at once, knowing what was going to happen.

"They're back again!" she shouted. This time both Sam and her mother heard her and came running in.

"There's going to be fires again," Laura shouted. "Please stop them!"

While her mother stood, bewildered, half-asleep still, Sam ran past her into his own room, pulled his clothes on over his pyjamas and ran outside. He yanked his bike out of the garden shed and raced like a small wind of fury down into the main street of the village.

"Fire!" he shouted. His voice echoed round the houses: "Fire!" even though there was no smoke or flames to be seen. People opened their doors and windows, wondering at his shouts, and as they came slowly out into the street they became aware of the sour smell of scorching, and the hiss of flames, and they turned round to see their curtains and carpets blazing behind them.

Laura and her mother stood at the window of Laura's bedroom. The houses in the valley were far below them, but they could hear the shouting as people ran out into the streets.

"You were right, Laura," her mother said. "There's more houses on fire."

But Laura had her head turned away from the flames, towards her own garden. The spicy smell had come back, and was far stronger than the bitter smoke fumes coming from the village. But she was aware of something else, and this was far more frightening and wonderful than anything else that had ever happened to her. Where her garden lay in its familiar quiet darkness something glowed. Deep in her mind's eye she could see it and she knew that it was white, like moonlight, with ripples of watery silver in it. But it wasn't just a colour. It was a shape. Something moving and living was in her garden, and it was looking at her with pale ice-blue eyes.

Sam was interviewed on local radio the next morning. It was a recorded interview, so he was sitting with Laura's family having breakfast when it was played. He beamed round at them all when he heard his name mentioned.

"Good morning! This is the breakfast news on your local radio station! Once more the small village of Ecclesham was subjected to an attack by unknown arsonists during the night. The alarm was raised by eleven-year-old Sam Totley…"

Here Laura touched Sam's arm so he would see that she was smiling at him.

"… whose own home was set alight the night before. He tells the story of how he saved his village to our reporter, Beverley Turner."

Then Sam's own voice came on, a bit breathless with nerves and excitement, but undeniably Sam's.

"I saw these lights moving down the hill. They were burning, like little fires on sticks, and there were lots of people carrying them…"

"You saw the arsonists, then?"

Sam's voice dropped a bit. "Well, I didn't exactly see all that. My friend did. She sees lots of things like that. She's blind, you see…"

The interviewer drew in her breath sharply. Sam hung his head at the table. Laura stretched her hand out to Sam to show she would have wanted him to say that. But her parents looked at each other across the table and sighed. Another of Laura's fancy stories.

"I see," the interviewer said, obviously puzzled. "Your friend will have heard them, then, Sam."

"Well, in her mind she saw them…"

"So what did you do?"

"I got my bike out of the shed and I rode down into the village. I just shouted as loud as I could to get everyone up. I didn't want anyone to get hurt you see…

like last night… my mum and dad had to go to hospital…"

"Yes, Sam. We know. So what d'you think you and your friend could tell us about these people who set fire to Ecclesham?"

"They came on horseback! One of them actually rode through her garden. Except, it didn't look like a horse hoofmark to me. As big as a horse… but different…"

Sam's voice was faded down and the news reporter's voice cut in. "And that was young Sam Totley, a brave lad who saved his village. It is estimated that the damage to the houses was something in the region of—"

Laura's dad switched the radio off.

"You were very good, Sam," Laura said.

"Thank you, Sam," Laura's mother said. "So we're going to have half the police in the county combing our back garden for hoofmarks!"

"What a pair of storytellers you are," Laura's father said. Laura knew this sort of voice of old. It meant that her father wasn't actually going to be angry and say he didn't believe them, but that he was going to chisel away at the story till he got to the "truth". "What did happen, Sam?"

"I told you… I ran out because Laura said she could hear men on wild horses. I just wanted to raise the alarm."

"Wild horses!" Laura's mother laughed. "I know you heard something, Laura. You were right to get Sam to raise the alarm. But we'd all have seen the horses! If there were any…"

"You must have smelt the smoke or something in your sleep. Good job you did," Laura's father suggested carefully. "But as for the horse in the garden…"

"It wasn't a horse," Sam said.

"I should think it wasn't," Laura's mother said. "How on earth would a horse get into our garden, Laura? Climb the wall, I suppose."

"It could have jumped," Laura said stubbornly. "Anyway, it was there. Last night… I saw it."

She clenched her hands together tightly, sensing the look her parents would be giving each other. Their silence lasted as long as it took her to unwrap her fingers and press them one by one on to the table-top. Her mother eased her hands up, pulling the tablecloth away to shake it out in the garden. Laura was disgraced now. They spoke as though she was no longer there.

"You don't have to believe everything Laura says, Sam," she heard her mother say. "She has a wonderful imagination. We call it her mind's eye."

"I know," Sam said. Now he was beginning to wonder whether to believe her or not. Laura could tell by the tone of his voice.

"Anyway," her father said, "the theory now is that the fires weren't caused by arsonists at all. There's no evidence of people having been near the place."

"Not even hoofmarks?" asked Sam. Laura kept her head down.

"No, Sam. Not even hoofmarks." Mr Brook pushed his chair away. He was getting ready to go to work. Normally at this time he'd have put his hand on Laura's shoulder, his signal for her to follow him out to the garage and listen till she heard his car turn the corner. He was going without his goodbye today, then.

Her mother followed him to the door. "What could it be, then? Some kind of internal combustion?" she asked.

"It's a possibility. Some freak condition of the building materials. All these houses are about the same age... That could explain why they're all setting alight at the same time."

"Good heavens, John." Mrs Brook half-laughed, with a stain of fear in her voice. "If that was true then ours could go up at any time. Tonight, even."

"Let's hope the danger's past, love." He kissed her lightly, closed the door, and went. Just as he reached his car his voice sang out. "Bye, Laura. Bye, Sam."

"Well," said Laura's mother. "I don't know what to think. But I ought to go down to the village to see if there's anything I can do – it's so depressing cleaning up a house after a fire – I remember when I set a chip pan on fire in the kitchen… that was bad enough. I thought I'd never get all that black off the walls and ceiling. You two will be all right for a bit won't you, up here?"

She went to Laura and sat down next to her, putting her arm round her. "Laura, Laura, what are we going to do with you? But you mustn't get upset when Dad goes off like that, my love." She rested her cheek against Laura's and hugged her. "I wish I could see into your mind's eye sometimes. Really see, I mean, not just hear your stories."

She smiled across at Sam, who was beginning to feel embarrassed. His mum never hugged him like that.

"Look after her, Sam. She's precious."

"Well, what shall we do?" Sam asked, after Laura's mum had gone out.

Laura kept her hands pressed down on the table, running just her thumbs along the edge. She knew every dent, and exactly where the wood underneath became rough because the varnish was wearing thin. This was what she did when she closed her mind against people. Sam found it unnerving.

"I thought I'd go for a ride on my bike," he said. "Just round about here. I've hardly ridden it yet."

Laura kept on rubbing and rubbing the edge of the table with her thumbs.

"You could have a go on it too, if you want. I'd push you round."

"I don't want to be pushed round on your bike."

"All right." He sat down opposite her. He wanted to grasp her hands and stop their movement, but he had never touched her, and didn't dare to. When she was like this she scared him. There was nothing in her eyes to show what she was feeling. He only knew she was upset and angry, and he didn't know what she wanted. "What do you want to do?"

"I want to go for a walk with Queenie," she said.

"All right," said Sam. "All right, if that's what you want to do. I'll have to come with you, though."

"No, you won't," said Laura. "I'm allowed to go out with Queenie."

Sam sighed. He could tell by Laura's voice that she was still hurt, and that she wanted to be on her own.

"Where d'you want to go, then?"

"Up the hill, of course. I want to go and find the men and their wild horses."

Chapter Four

SNATCHED

LAURA WAITED TILL she heard Sam opening the shed door
and wheeling his bike away before she and Queenie went
out into the garden. She was upset and bewildered. For a
long time now she'd relied on Sam to see for her, and
they had shared everything. He told her what he could
see in front of his eyes, and she told him what she could
see behind hers. They understood each other. He had
never doubted her before. Now she felt alone. She knelt

down to stroke Queenie, and tried to remember back to a time before she knew Sam, to a little girl time when she had been able to see dimly with her own eyes, before she had gone fully blind. That had been a frightening period when lights had danced and flickered so confusingly that she used to cry for night to come.

In those days she used to pretend to herself that she was really two people, and one of them could see and the other couldn't. They used to whisper together in their shadow-light and help each other. She called one Laura and the other Midnight, and she was never sure which one of them she really was. Her mother and father didn't know about Midnight. They used to watch Laura when she was a little girl, sitting with her hands spread out in front of her eyes, talking to herself, and they wondered what she could see that they couldn't.

And one day her mother had taken her to the hospital and had come home worried and unhappy. Laura's eyes were hurt and dazzling with the lights the doctors had shone into them, but her mother had taken her to her room and held her up to the mirror.

"Look," she had said. "That's your face. Always remember it."

Laura could remember what she had seen then: the dimly swirling colours of her own face and eyes and hair. Though the pictures had hurt she had held out her hands to the mirror, and the child in the mirror had held out her hands to Laura. "Midnight!" Laura had laughed, and her mother had brought the child's head down to nestle in the warmth of her own hair, rocking her gently and sadly. "You're a midnight child, Laura," she had whispered to her. "And soon you'll live in a dark, dark world." As her mother had rocked her from side to side Laura had peered again at the moving patches of pale light and soft colours that were the reflection of her own face, and her own smile had dazzled back at her. When she was alone that night she had giggled to Midnight: "I've seen you!" and they whispered together about the ghost-flickerings of her face.

And soon the lights stopped coming at all. In a way it was comforting, that shadowland of blindness. There were no bright lights to confuse or frighten her. She didn't need Midnight any more. That part of herself faded away.

Queenie whimpered, and Laura stood up.

"I need you now, Midnight," she whispered. "What is it that comes to my garden? See for me!" She peered into the dark tunnel of her blindness, sensing a soft movement in the grass, and warm breath on her outstretched hand, and a waft of sweet air.

The creature had come back.

"Please let me see you!" Laura begged.

The air seemed to flicker round her and then grew still again. Queenie, sensing nothing, pulled impatiently at her lead, and at last Laura followed her, feeling for the latch and letting the gate slam shut behind her.

Sam had wheeled his bike out of the garden and then had stood waiting to see what Laura would do. He would have liked to cycle down into the village to see if Tim and Ian were all right, but didn't know whether Laura was supposed to go out on her own with her dog.

"'Course she is!" he told himself. "That's what guide dogs are for." He swung his leg round over the back of the saddle. "But Queenie isn't a guide dog," he reminded himself. "She's just an ordinary labrador. Laura told me that you have to be eighteen to have a proper guide dog. So Queenie won't have been properly trained. She'll stay by Laura's side, but will she know how to find the safest paths for her?"

Yet Laura and Queenie often went out together on the path behind her house. He'd seen them. They probably knew every step of the way by heart.

He cycled to the end of the road, and stopped.

"She never goes far, though. Up on that hill, with all those rocks and slippery paths, anything could happen. And what if there really are wild horses up there?"

He started to cycle back to the house again and then swerved round. He knew the story of the horses wasn't true. He'd have seen them when he rode down into the village, wouldn't he? He sighed. Laura was a strange one. Sometimes he thought he knew her better than anyone, and sometimes he didn't know her at all.

He could just see her now, her long hair swinging as she mounted the ridge at the top of the hill and stood resting with her arm propped against a boulder. He could see Queenie's white tail wagging, looking up to Laura for a sign to move on. Then Laura took a step forward and suddenly knelt down; or maybe she'd stumbled. It was hard to tell.

"Look after her," Laura's mum had said. "She's precious."

Sam rode at full speed to Laura's house, clanked his bike into the garage, and then started up the hillside after her.

Wayfinder was crouched on the edge of the hill. The Old Woman came up to him and put her hand on his shoulder.

"Is it nearly darkfall yet?" she asked.

"Not yet time, Old Woman. The sun's hardly halfway round the sky."

The Old Woman crouched next to him. "There's mystery about," she said. "Can you hear mansounds, Wayfinder? Catch eyesight. Give me wordspeak of them."

"There's a manfolk beast, and a girlchild."

"A girlchild, eh?" She sucked in through her teeth. "Give me word-pictures."

"She has long bright hair and white skin. She walks slow, as if her eyes see darkness."

The Old Woman drew in her breath sharply. "Go on."

Wayfinder leaned forward again.

"And down in the dipdown a boychild's following her."

Sloe ran to them, gasping for breath.

"Menfolk coming, Old Woman," he panted. "Take hiding-places."

The Old Woman stood up and shook her head. "Hide from the boychild if you can. And the manfolk beast. But there's mystery about that girlchild, be sure of that. She knows us. She's the one who's keeping us from our Wilderness. And my Spellhorn."

Laura knew the way up the hillside very well. She and Queenie often went up there with her father. It was a good walk for her because there was a clear path with trees on each side for most of the way, and she could hear the leaves rustling and reach out and touch the trunks if she wanted to check how far she'd gone. But once she came above the tree-line the wind always rushed raw at her. She didn't like it up there; there was nothing for her to touch till she reached the very top, with its rough-skinned, familiar boulders.

Today she made her way steadily, and leaned against the big top boulder to catch her breath. The wind was cold and sharp. Queenie sat down patiently beside her; then, as soon as she stepped forward, went with her. After a few paces Laura stopped and knelt down, feeling round on the ground for hoofmarks. She stood up and went forward and knelt again, and then again. And at last she found them, scuffed into the soft earth. She leaned right back on her heels, thinking, and Queenie lay beside her, ears cocked, watching her.

Now Laura could smell the charred bitter-sweet smell of burnt wood. As her breathing quietened down she could hear, so faint at first that she couldn't be sure it was there at all, the stamping of restless hooves, and the snortings and blowings of horses. She could hear the soft whisper of men talking together in a strange lilting tongue, and the sound of something like logs being dragged along. And, so faint that it was hardly there, she heard something creeping up to her, very slowly, on all fours. Some kind of animal, perhaps. She felt the tickle-touch of hair on her skin as the creature moved near her face. She could smell the rank breath of the Old Woman, crouched right up to her with her hair loose and wafting. She sensed her, peering without seeing, deep into her own eyes.

"Laura!"

The sounds and smells vanished.

"Laura. Are you all right?" Sam ran up to her and knelt by her. Queenie sprang up and came between them, trying to lick them both.

"I decided to come up with you after all. D'you want to carry on?"

"No thanks, Sam." Laura stood up and pulled Queenie's lead. "There's no point. They've gone."

The Old Woman and Sideman waited in the boulders till Laura and Sam were out of sight.

"That girlchild has mind-eye," the Old Woman said. "She knows us."

"She didn't get eyeful of us," Sideman told her. "Nor did her dog get noseful of us, nor did the boy get earful."

"But she knows us. Seek her shelter come moontime, Wayfinder. That's where my Spellhorn has his hiding-hole, be sure of that. If anyone can cradle him, and gentle him down to be snatched away, that girlchild can. This night we'll have him back with us, and our home way to the Wilderness will be safe found." She bent her back, shifting the weight of her years from one leg to the other. "But he'll never leave the girlchild now. Snatch her too."

Laura was fidgety all evening. No one could get a word out of her, yet she was trembly inside herself. At last her mother told her to do something, and she went to her cupboard and brought out her typewriter. She put it on the table where Sam was drawing a picture of Queenie. He watched her as she fed a sheet of stiff brown paper into it.

"What're you doing?" he asked her.

"Typing," she said. "Can't you tell?"

"It doesn't look like a typewriter to me," Sam said. "It's hardly got any keys."

"It's a Perkins."

"Perk something then."

She smiled and quickly pressed down some of the keys, then drew out the brown sheet. She handed it to him, and he ran his finger over the small pinprick holes punched in it.

"Is it braille?" he asked. "I can't feel any difference in them. How d'you do it?"

She shrugged. She wasn't really in the mood for talking.

"What does it say?" Sam asked.

"Guess."

He studied it.

It was difficult to tell where one letter would end and the next would begin. He found a pencil and copied the pattern of dots carefully on to a piece of paper.

"Well, it's two words, and I think they've both got five letters."

"Brilliant," said Laura. "You can count."

"Don't be like that," said Sam. "It doesn't look anything like our writing, you know. Two of the letters in the first word are the same, if they are letters. They're just a dot. The second letter and the fifth letter."

"Go on," said Laura. "And are any of the other letters alike?"

"Yes! The third and fourth letters of the second word are the same as each other. Three dots each, like sideways triangles. Oh yes… and there's some more. The fourth letter in the first word is the same as the second letter in the second word." He ran his finger over the dots again and shook his head. "I give in," he said at last.

But Laura had lost interest. She sat drumming her fingers on the table until her mother made her stop.

"Laura Brook!" she shouted. "Enough is enough! I don't know what's up with you tonight!"

Laura went up to her room. Downstairs she could hear Sam punching away on her Perkins. She opened her window. Nothing there. Nothing to hear. Nothing to smell. But something in the air that was as jittery as a hive of bees.

"Is it moon-up yet?" the Old Woman called.

Sideman crawled to her. "Soon come," he told her. "The birds are shutting eyes, and the owls are round about. All the manfolk shelters in the dipdown have orange lights glowing."

"And the girlchild's shelter? Have you wayfound it?"

"We have, Old Woman. Wayfinder sniffed it out. There's a flowerden there."

"That's where he'll be!" She chortled. Her fingers cracked as she rubbed her hands together. "That's his hiding-hole, be sure!"

That night Laura couldn't get to sleep. As soon as she heard her parents going upstairs and turning off the lights she got out of bed and found her jacket and shoes. She made her way quietly downstairs. Queenie nosed up to her in the kitchen and Laura knelt down and hugged her, letting the dog nuzzle right into her neck and her hair.

"You're my best friend, my best friend, Queenie," she told her. "How I wish I could see you." The dog whined and licked inside her ear, and Laura laughed and pushed her back down into her basket.

"Now you stay there, good girl," she whispered. "I want to be on my own." She stood up slowly; sad, and not understanding why. She put her hands out to feel for the bolts on the door, opened it, and went out.

Wind rustled the trees and grasses, like a voice sighing between the house and the garage. A quick flurry of leaves scratched against the bin. As Laura stepped down from the concrete steps on to the lawn she could hear the soft grass squelch beneath her feet. She reached out and touched the knobbly bark of the first apple tree, then the second, and went past them into her own small garden. She could smell the freshly turned earth, and the figgy smell of old leaves. The wind was cold on her face. She pulled up the collar of her jacket and dug her hands into her pockets, and waited.

The scent came first. It was deep and spicy and sweet, exactly as she'd remembered it. She stayed tight still. Then she heard the rustle and crack of twigs being stepped on, and the soft swish of grass, and the crumble of earth, and then silence. Close to her she felt the wary, still presence of a creature in her garden.

"Come here," she whispered.

The creature lifted a hoof nervously, then stayed still again. Laura strained forward, hands stretched out in front of her. Her breath was bursting in her lungs in case she frightened the timid thing away. The tips of her fingers touched silky hair. She drew her hands slowly away and stood still, letting her breath out inch by inch. The creature was right in front of her.

In twos and threes, furtive as foxes, the Wild Ones crept down the hillside towards Laura's house. In front came Sideman, leading the Old Woman by a touch on her arm. As soon as they reached flat ground they loped along on all fours, like long-backed beasts. Behind the gang came the women, leading the horses, step by quiet step. In the hush of shadows they lurked round the dark garden.

"We have him!" the Old Woman breathed. "Let the child gentle him for us."

Laura crouched down, holding one hand out. "Ssh!" she whispered. "It's all right, creature. Come to me."

The creature lifted a hoof again and softly stepped forward.

Again Laura felt the silky touch of hair against her fingertips. This time she stroked the creature's warm side, very gently, coaxing him with whispers, till at last he sank down like a foal in the grass and put his head on her lap.

"Snatch him!" the Old Woman sang out.

That was the moment when the world lit up for Laura. She saw the night garden, bluey-black as damsons, and the deep green of leaves. She saw the navy sky clustered with the brilliant lights of stars. She saw the creature, silvery-white-haired, with a pearly horn between his ice-blue eyes. And she saw the long-haired men beasts come leaping at her, laughing, out of the shadows.

The smallest of them, an old woman beast, white-haired and crease-skinned, darted forward and clasped the creature round the neck. He struggled up again, twisting his head round to keep his eyes fixed on Laura.

"Wayfind us to the Wilderness, Spellhorn," the Old Woman laughed. "We're heartsad for home, old silverback." Laura stepped forward, desperate not to lose him, and felt the Old Woman's clawed fingers grasping her arm. "Clamber up!" she told her. "Spellhorn needs you, Girlchild!"

And this was what Sam saw as he ran out into the garden, drowsy with sleep. He saw a team of shaggy grey horses with long-haired creatures crouching on their backs. He saw a unicorn leaping the low wall by the apple trees. On his back, laughing with joy, he saw an old she-creature, her white hair streaming behind her. And he saw Laura clinging to her.

"Laura! Laura! Come back!" Sam ran to the shed and hauled his bike out, and set up a desperate chase up the hillside, weaving in and out of the cantering horses, his wheels choking up with grass, with the wild laughter and the stamping of hooves ringing in his ears.

And then they vanished, from sight, from sound. The hillside was sleeping quiet again. Laura, and the Wild Ones, and the unicorn, had gone.

Chapter Five

AWAY WITH THE WILD ONES

BUT LAURA DIDN'T see Sam. Behind her was blackness. If she'd turned her head at all as the Wild Ones thundered up the hill, she would have seen nothing but blank darkness. But ahead of her the sky was flashing with stars, and the moon was a deep white pool.

The Old Woman was hunched up in front of her, knees drawn up, back bent, her gnarled hands gripping the unicorn's horn. She was chuckling, deep down inside her, chuckling like a broody hen with glee. The unicorn soon streamed ahead of the heavy horses with its long, even stride. The Old Woman's coarse hair lashed against Laura's face and stung her eyes; strands of it whipped across her mouth, so she had to keep spitting it away. Her arms ached as she clung to the bent body. If she let go, she knew she'd tumble backwards into the path of the horses pounding behind them. And still the unicorn galloped on, like a swift boat cutting through water.

Laura gulped the cold flow of air. "Where are we going?" she shouted.

"Homeland." The Old Woman laughed out loud now. "At longlast time we're heading for homeland."

"Where's that?" Laura asked.

"Old home, earth home, birth home of all the Wild Ones." The Old Woman urged the unicorn on even faster, thrilled by the thoughts of going home. "Hurry us there, Spellhorn."

Laura had to be content with that. The wind smashed like waves against her face. She buried her head down into the Old Woman's hunched back, and concentrated on hanging on.

They had come to a stream that cut its way deep into the moors, bubbling up and then seeping down again underground. The Old Woman clicked in the hollow of her throat and the unicorn slackened its pace and danced to a halt. Wayfinder leant across to help Laura down. She felt dizzy with the speed. Her legs would hardly hold her. She sank to the ground, weak and cold. When the Old Woman slid off his back, Spellhorn trotted round and put his head down to Laura, nudging her gently so the silky, beardy strands under his chin tickled her cheek. She could feel the warm breath from his nostrils.

The horses rolled over in the grass, glad to be rid of their riders, kicking their legs in the air, and then stepped down to the stream. They dipped their noses into it and drank thirstily, sucking up the water in long draughts through their teeth. And one by one the Wild Ones loped across to Laura. They clustered round her, staring like children, muttering words that she could only just understand. Some of them dropped down on to all fours to get a better look at her, and crept right up to her face as if they were trying to sniff her. The old Wild Man stood in front of her and glared.

"You should never have snatched her, Old Woman." His voice growled like an old dog's. "She'll never no time be one of us."

The Old Woman took one of his hands in her own and patted it. "She's readynow one of us, I'd say," she said. "Look how the unicorn is heartful of her."

Laura felt lonely and frightened. She reached up and stroked the unicorn's nose.

"Why did you do this to me, unicorn?" she whispered. "You tricked me! You knew I'd be captured."

The unicorn whinnied, trembling the fine hairs round his nostrils.

"Take eyeful of her!" the old man rumbled. "She even tries to give Spellhorn scoldspeak!"

The Wild Ones laughed, baring their yellow teeth and biffing each other gently with cuffed fists, then turned back to the stream, crouching so they could lower their heads into it and sip.

A young one squatted down next to Laura and nudged her.

"Don't be downsad," he whispered. "There's right many seegood things in the Wilderness. You'll be gladful to be there."

"Will I?" Laura sniffed. She felt a bit better now, though her legs and arms were still aching. She risked a look at the Wild Boy. He peered at her through a mass of rough and stringy hair, but his face was friendly. His cheeks bulged when he smiled. "Have you got a name?" she asked him.

"My newborn name is Sloe," he told her. He turned round and pointed to two Wild Ones who were rubbing each other's hands to get warm. "Take eyeful of them. He's Wayfinder, and she's Water, and I'm the carechild of them. They give me motherfatherlove. You too, Girlchild, if you'll let them do that thing."

"I'm not Girlchild. I'm Laura."

Sloe laughed, drawing back his lips to show his clenched teeth, as the others had done. "Laura is a makesmile born name," he said. "But I'll live with it."

"And who's the very old growly one?" Laura asked. The old man was crouched by the stream, drinking with loud slurps. When he glanced round to scowl at Sloe water trickled down his matted beard.

"I name him Shrivel-skin," Sloe whispered. "But I keep that hidden in my head-hole. He grumps a lot these days. But his real Wild One name is Sideman. He stands at the side of the Old Woman when she gives us wordspeak. And he's her lovingfriend."

Wayfinder called Sloe over to him to help him gather the horses back, and Laura watched the boy scamper away, clicking in his throat as he went.

"Too soon for sleeptime, slackbones," Wayfinder shouted to the horses. "Wait till sun-up for that, when we've found us some hiding-holes."

"We'll have halt for bellyfill soon," the Old Woman said. She hauled herself up on to Spellhorn's back and jerked her head for Laura to do the same. "But let's dash on now."

Laura had hardly settled herself back on to the unicorn when he plunged forward, mane and tail floating out like strands of pale thread. Behind her the Wild Ones grunted to their horses to urge them on. The hooves rumbled on the stony ground, echoing between boulders, making the earth below them sound like hollow iron. Sideman caught up with them, crouched so low on his horse that his hair tangled in its mane, the same colour, the same coarse thickness. He roared at it to make it go faster and still faster, and the Old Woman chuckled and kicked the unicorn's sides with her bare heels.

Laura turned her head away from Sideman. Sloe was catching up with them on the other side, his face wild and laughing, loving the speed.

"Be heartful, Girlchild," he shouted. "Bellyfill soon, and then the shuteye time. And after that, the battlebite of the unicorns! Safekeep!"

Chapter Six

GIRLCHILD AND OLD BONES

SAM DRAGGED HIS bike back down the hill. Laura's mother and father had come running out of the house and were anxiously calling him back in.

"Sam! Come back here!" Mr Brook shouted. "What d'you think you're doing?"

Sam was nearly crying. "They've taken Laura away."

"Laura's in bed," Mr Brook said. "And so should you be. Come on."

"But she isn't in bed," Sam insisted. Mr Brook had taken his bike off him and was half-carrying it down towards the gate. Sam stumbled after him. "Please listen, Mr Brook. I think Laura's been kidnapped."

"Kidnapped!" Mr Brook smiled down at him and tousled his hair.

"They were people on horses. Shaggy horses. People with long hair… they didn't look like people… they were all shouting… and there was a little old one… it grabbed Laura… it wasn't riding a horse… it was a kind of a… a kind of a… I think it was a unicorn."

Sam knew he wasn't talking properly. His face was turned up to Mr Brook's and he was shouting and crying but the words were coming out like bubbles, all in a floating jostling rush, and they were bouncing off Mr Brook's surprised and frowning face and bursting into splashes of nonsense.

"Calm down, Sam," said Mr Brook quietly. "Let's get you back in the house."

Sam followed him back into the garden and watched him tuck his bike away. He felt numb and shocked; his legs were aching with the effort of trying to drive his pedals uphill across grass, and he was shivering with cold and fright. Laura's mum came over and put her arms round him.

"Poor Sam," she said. "He's still shocked from that fire."

"I… tried to stop… them." His breath was coming in huge gasps.

"Nothing's happened, Sam. It's all right. There's no horses. Laura's fast asleep. Just come in and get warm. Come on now."

Mrs Brook tucked a warm, heavy coat round Sam's shoulders and knelt down by him.

"Listen, Sam. Laura has a very strange imagination. She makes things up all the time; she has a little fantasy world that she lives in, where she sees things that we can't see. That's all right. It's only fair in a way, I suppose. But the trouble is, she tries to make other people believe in it too. You have to be firm with her, and tell her it's all in her mind's eye. Whatever you saw out there was in your mind, that's all. You mustn't let these things frighten you."

Sam felt dizzy. He could still hear the thundering of hooves as the heavy horses had ploughed up the hill. He could feel the cold wind they stirred up as they swept past him, and how it had made his bicycle sway. He could hear the rough voices shouting and laughing.

"They were there," he said, and his voice was tight and small and tired in his throat. He'd rather go to bed than have to think about all this. "In your garden. I saw them."

"Sam," said Mrs Brook. "We have a tiny lawn, and a few apple trees. We have a little path and some steps. How could the garden be full of horses?"

"But it was."

Mrs Brook put out the light and held out her hand for him to follow her upstairs. "Come on, Sam."

"But we've got to find Laura!" He tried to stop the tears of frustration coming.

"That's all right," Mrs Brook said. "We're going to find her now. I'm going to take you up to her room and show you where she's been all this time, fast asleep in her bed. Come on."

It was a cold, misty dawn by the time the Wild Ones stopped again. Laura was nearly asleep on the unicorn's back, rocked up and down with the motion of his speeding. It seemed to her that someone lifted her down and carried her across uneven, rocky ground; she couldn't be sure. All she knew was that when she woke up properly she was curled up by a crackling fire, and that the Wild One called Water was watching her anxiously.

"You've had the good shuteye," she laughed.

Laura sat up slowly, bewildered and uneasy again. She'd dreamt that she'd been in her own bed, and that her mother had come into the room with Sam to wake her up. She remembered Sam's puzzled, worried voice as he'd spoken her name, but in her dream she'd reached out to touch them both, spreading out her fingers as far as they would go. And there'd been nothing there.

Water touched Laura's cheek, and then clucked softly in her throat. "There's raindrops in your eyes," she said. "Don't be woeful, Girlchild." She made a comforting sort of ringing, purring sound in her throat, and rocked her head from side to side. The unicorn picked his way over the rough ground, delicate as a goat, and grazed quietly near their feet. Laura knelt up to stroke him. The colours around her dazzled and bewildered her. When she had first seen Spellhorn in her garden he had been silvery like the moonlight. Now he glowed red-gold with the fluttering light from the fire. When she looked round her she could see the eyes of the Wild Ones watching her, and they were like the burning nuts of wood in the flames, gleaming with sparks. Their faces shone in the yellow light, and some of them wore rich blood-red or earth-brown robes that had the lustre of the firelight in their folds, and their long hair drifted out like flames as they moved.

"Here, Girlchild." Sloe crept over to her with a pot bowl cupped in his hands. "Here's your bellyfill," he said. "Have it hot."

Laura took the bowl gratefully, balancing it with the tips of both her thumbs and first fingers. It was very hot because it had been cooked in the flames of the big fire, and lifted out with stones.

"What is it?" she asked. The steam from it warmed her face.

"Mush," said Sloe. "And right good, too."

When it was cool enough to eat Laura managed to sip at it. It seemed to be a kind of porridge made with oats and fruit; the taste reminded her a little of cherries and bananas and bread and honey and milk, and yet it wasn't really like any of these things.

But it was good, and warming, and the more she supped it the stronger she felt. She found herself lapping it up greedily, the way Water and Sloe were eating theirs, and licking out the bowl with her tongue. At last she put it down with a deep contented sigh, and saw them both cuffing each other with laughter.

"Right good bellyfill," she said, and laughed with them.

Sloe scampered away with the bowl, and Water curled up by the fire to doze off. Laura looked round her. She was still confused by the brightness of everything, and by the startling colours of the sky and the trees. She held up her hands and spread them out wide. She clenched up her fists and opened out her fingers again, slowly this time, one by one. She looked with wonder at the tiny lines on the palms of her hands and the fine hairs on the backs of her fingers, and the curved shiny shells of her nails. Then she pressed her hands against her eyes, letting the world go dark again. She tilted her head back and saw the red light of day filtering through the bars of her fingers, as if the sun was glowing inside her skin and bones. She laughed out loud and gazed round her again, smiling at the way the leaves fluttered like small green suns over her head.

She had no idea where she was, except that they seemed to be in a rough clearing inside a wood. She could hear sharp cracks, and the sound of beating. The Wild Ones were breaking up twigs and branches to feed their fires, and some of them were using sticks to thrash through the undergrowth, making little hollow dens under bushes, that they could crawl inside.

Laura wondered how safe it would be for her to try and escape. Her dreams of Sam and her mother lingered, leaving her still uneasy and sad. Maybe it would be possible for her to get back home, if she could get out of the woods.

"Girlchild." A dry voice crackled into her thoughts, and she realised that the Old Woman had been sitting on the other side of the fire and watching her all the time. "Come and talk to Old Bones here."

"I don't want to talk to you," Laura said. "I don't understand why you've brought me here. And I want to go home."

All the same, she found herself standing up and going over to where the Old Woman was crouched. As soon as she moved, Spellhorn lifted up his head from his grazing and followed her round. The Old Woman held out her hand to him, and he nuzzled into her soft palm.

"My reckoning is that you'll be heartglad in the Wilderness," the Old Woman told Laura.

"But where is the Wilderness?" Laura asked.

The Old Woman chuckled. "That's a makethink one," she said. "But maybe the Wilderness isn't a Where Is Place at all."

"Then what is it?"

"Maybe it's a When Was Time." The Old Woman nodded at Laura. "That's the Wilderness."

"What d'you mean?"

The Old Woman scratched her head with her long curved nails. "Wilderness is the time-began thing. Wilderness is the young world, long ago quiet. You'll have heart's ease there, all right."

Laura thought about this, while the Old Woman watched her and Spellhorn snuffled round her feet for fresh grass.

"If it's so good," Laura said at last, "why did you bother coming out? And why did you come to our village? And why did you kidnap me?"

The Old Woman clapped her hands together. The firelight flames danced in her nut-brown eyes. "Many why-whys!" she laughed. "I'll have to look deep in my brainbox to find becauses." She scratched her head again.

"Well, Spellhorn wayfound your shelter, that's one thing sure, but he didn't give us the why-why because he hasn't got a wordbox in his mouth."

She chuckled again. "But from time to time through the long years of menfolk the Wild Ones take wanderlust. We're nosy to see what menfolk has got up to. It makes us heartsad, too, sometimes," she said. "We see the nice world going dumpy. Bad smells all over the air. Loud noises scraping our earholes. Menfolk make things rusty, and scratched, and uglydumps. They don't look after it right, that's sad. And they don't look after each other right good, neither."

She shook her head, and sat with her arms hugging her legs and her knees pulled right up to her chin, staring into the fire.

"The unicorn gives us eyebright and helps us see these things. You have eyebright too, Girlchild. That's your special thing."

"I was blind till the unicorn came," Laura said. "Now I can see everything."

"That's all many thanks to the unicorn's mystery power," the Old Woman told her. "Be good to him, or you'll have nightdark back." She turned her head sideways to look at Laura. "Can you see the earth colours and the flower lights, sky shinings and all?"

Laura nodded, and the Old Woman wagged her finger

at her. "That's not the half of it," she said. "Hang on for the Wilderness, Girlchild. It's all time-began colours there, all newborn – so full of shimmerings it'll make your heart grow big enough to pop. You'll see."

Spellhorn came to kneel between them and the Old Woman tickled his ears fondly. "Spellhorn sought you out, Girlchild. He wanted you, know that."

"But why?"

"Oh, that's not for telling yet. We'll find out soon. I always keep-mind the day Spellhorn found me," she said. "Shall I give you the tell tale of it?"

"Yes, please," said Laura.

The Old Woman kept her voice as low as the flickerings of the flames, so it was a story just for Laura while the Wild Ones went about their jobs. "Longtime longtime there were Wild Wars. Not Wild Ones against Wild Ones, know that. That thing never happens. But our Wilderness was tackled from the air, by bats!"

"Bats!" said Laura. "How could they harm you?"

The Old Woman blew out her cheeks. "Moonbats!" she said. She spread her arms wide to show the size of them.

"Huge moonbats came to put evil into Wild Ones' hearts, and many Wild Ones died. My motherfatherfolk took their last sleep then, and I was heartsad. And day had turned to night for me because of the flashings of the moonbat wings. They stole my eyelight away. Then Spellhorn found me. I caught scent of him first, and when I gentled him to kneel by me he let me clamber on his back. And then I had eyebright again, Girlchild, just like you. He brought me safekeep to the Wilderness place, and I knew he'd stay with me all days. And he did, till he came for you. He brought us out of the Wilderness, and we didn't know what for. And off he went to a hiding-place, and we were heartsad. My eyebright grew dim again, and we thought we must stay away from our Wilderness for ever. And then he found you." The Old Woman chuckled, patting Laura's hands. "And I'm right heartglad, too. You've got mystery, Girlchild, and that's good for Wild Ones."

She yawned suddenly, letting out a long rasping sigh of breath. "Now get some shuteye," she said. "They'll have given the bushes a thwack to find you a hiding-hole. This drizzledown will put the fires out soon, and there's the battlebite to face at dusk."

"What happens then?" asked Laura.

The Old Woman hunched her shoulders into a shrug. "Badthing, goodthing, who guesses?" she said. "Only knowthing is that the hornless ones will seek us out soon, that's sure."

"Who are they?"

"They're unicorns without horns. They had their horns stole off by greedy menfolk way way back. Menfolk always want their spellhorns, their mysteries. But once the horn is stole away, the unicorn is waylost, evermore. These hornless ones wander here, woeful deep in hearts. They're alltime landlocked in these Bad Woods. No Wilderness down here, no way."

"And what happens at the battlebite?"

The Old Woman blew out her cheeks. "They're evil in their mind-holes these days, that's one thing sure. Their only thinking is to stop us going to the Wilderness too. They'll do battlebite with Spellhorn to stop him going back." She opened her hands wide, showing the soft pink palms, and placed them over Spellhorn's eyes. "That's shuteye time, for gathering of strength," she whispered to him. "For all of us, good shuteye now."

"But I've already had a sleep," Laura began. The Old Woman yawned again and slowly rolled over on to her side like a cat, pulling her blanket of white hair over herself. She snored deeply. Sideman crawled over to her on all fours and lay down next to her, tucking his fists into his eye-holes to keep the daylight out, and soon he, too, began to rumble steadily.

Laura stood up. Under the bushes and all round her the Wild Ones lay in small hairy bundles like animals, snoring and sighing. Rain fizzed in the flames. The horses coughed and hung their heads low, dozing. Only the unicorn watched her, his eyes the only living thing in his still body. And deep in her head, far, far away, Laura heard Sam's voice calling her name.

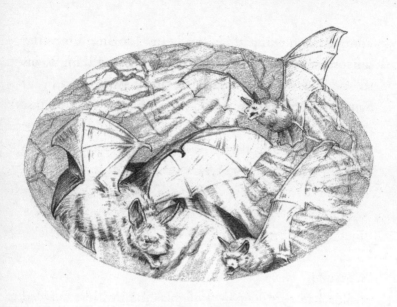

Chapter Seven

THE MOONBATS

SAM WAS KNEELING on the deep windowsill of his bedroom, staring out into the dark garden. Laura's mother and father were talking loudly in the next room, arguing about Laura.

"She can't have gone out on her own!" Laura's father was saying. "She wouldn't. She must be in the house somewhere."

"I've looked, haven't I?" Mrs Brook shouted, a sharp edge of panic in her voice. "She's not in the house, John."

"Then where is she?" Sam heard Mr Brook running downstairs. "You search the garden, Susan. I'll go down the hill. She won't be far off. Get Sam to help."

But Sam stayed in his room, pressing his head against the damp windowglass. He knew it was no use to look for Laura in the garden or in the village or even on the hills up above the valley. Wherever she was, it was somewhere that her parents would never reach.

"Laura," he said, so quietly that the sound was only a thought in his head. "Come back to us."

"Girlchild!"

Sloe had read Laura's thoughts. She had just crawled back away from the sleeping Wild Ones and had started to run through the woods, letting the brambles scratch her legs and arms. As soon as Sloe woke up he jumped lightly to his feet and like a swift deer came streaking after her.

The branches seemed to swirl round her, reaching fingers down to catch her. She closed her eyes. For a moment she didn't know whether she was awake or in a dream, in her own soft bed or stumbling through tearing brambles. She didn't know whether the voice that was calling her was Sam's or Sloe's. She tried to run faster, but her legs wouldn't move. She had no idea which way to turn.

"Girlchild!" Sloe jumped out on to the path in front of her, crouching with his knees bent and his arms stretched out to stop her going any further. "No time now for wanderlust!" he told her. "This is the shuteye time before the night-time's battlebite."

"I'm not tired," she tried to say, but then she realised that she was tired, almost too tired to stand up or to keep her eyes open. She allowed Sloe to lead her back to where the Wild Ones lay snoring. He took her right up to where the unicorn stood quietly waiting and watching as though he knew every thought in her mind, and left her there. Laura knelt down by Spellhorn. She was heavy with drowsiness. He lowered his head down to her.

"I can't stay with you, Spellhorn," she sighed. He knelt down by her and she stroked his silky mane. Her eyelids drooped. Little by little her head sank down till it was resting on his warm, soft side, and she fell asleep.

The Wild Ones woke up gradually all round her, snorting and grunting and licking their dry lips. The Old Woman kicked Sideman awake, and he spat into the ashes of their fire and shuffled off to waken the grubwomen and the flamefinders.

"Gather wet berries and sweetnuts and mushplants," he growled. "Old Bones wants berry juice bake for her bellyfill."

By the time dusk came the fires were crackling high again. The Wild Ones ate noisily, shouting and laughing after their long, good sleep. They let Laura sleep on. The unicorn still knelt wide-eyed beside her, calm in all that rioting. Wayfinder bent some twigs and stretched wiry bindweed tight across them to make a kind of small harp. He stroked it with his long nails, sending a ripple of soft sound over the talk and laughter. Water hummed. Laura opened his eyes and lay still, listening. The Old Woman clicked quietly in her throat and Sloe sidled round to her.

"Did the girlchild head for backhome?" she whispered.

Sloe nodded.

"No shock to me," she said. "But good watcheye, Sloe, to bring her safekeep back."

"She was wearylegs," he said. "And all eyedroop."

The Old Woman looked sideways at him. "You like her, Sloe? Are you heartglad to have her with us? Eh?"

Sloe covered his face with his hands. "Maybe nodhead, maybe shakehead," he muttered through his fingers.

The Old Woman clenched up her fists and tapped her knuckles together in time to Wayfinder's music. "She gives you eyebright, that's sure," she chuckled. "Open your ears to me, Sloe. One time faraway the girlchild could be your alltime friend. Like Sideman and Old Bones. Know that!"

Sloe rocked backwards and forwards on the balls of his feet, his hands still covering his face. Flight glanced across at them, frowning, and the Old Woman stuck out her bottom teeth and lip at her to make her turn away.

"The girlchild still has heartwishings for home," she said. "But if she goes, the unicorn will follow her and the Wild Ones will be waylost once more. This is your job for me, boy Sloe. Come moon-up, when the howl-wolf creeps in the shadowings and the noises of the night shriek out loud, keep your eyes open for her. Safekeep!"

Soon it was dark. Laura sat up and edged herself back away from the unicorn. He stood up, watching her. It seemed to Laura that all the Wild Ones were asleep again, lying in still deep-breathing bundles. But she was wide awake, and felt sure that she had the strength to get right out of the woods before daybreak. She tiptoed away from the glow of the fires, startling herself with the sharp cracks the twigs made under her feet. Huge dark shapes fluttered up into the trees and hunched themselves upside down in high branches, and it seemed to her that they were watching her, turning their heads to follow her as she moved. From somewhere deep in the woods came a long shivering howl. Yet still the unicorn was watching her. She was torn between staying with him and running for her freedom.

She made herself move forward. A small beast moaned in near bushes. An owl screeched. The dark humps in the branches rippled leathery wings. Then she heard the dry shuffling of light footsteps, and she knew that she was being followed. Something reached out and touched her arm.

"Who is it?" she gasped.

"Your one time alltime good friend," Sloe whispered, close to her ear. "No time for running backhome, Girlchild."

She struggled away from him. "You must let me go," she said. "How can I stay with the Wild Ones, Sloe?"

"No running free here," he whispered again. "Take earful, Girlchild. There's night beasts all around."

Laura listened. Soft steps prowled round them, steady and slow.

"The unicorns of darkness are creeping tiptoe through the shadowness," Sloe breathed. "The Wild Ones are lying wide-eyed and ear-stretched, waiting for this pounce. It's near time for the battlebite."

Suddenly there was a huge whooshing of air as the black bat shapes lifted up from their tree shades. As they spread out, the sky lit up with the dazzling lights of their underwings. They flashed like white flames, twitching and swerving round their heads.

"Close up your eyecovers!" Sloe shouted. "They'll burn your eyes out." He tucked his head down under his arm and tugged at Laura. "Scuttle for shelter before they snatch us up!"

Laura ran after him with her head well down.

"Crouch in there, where the tree arms make a cave!" Sloe shouted. He pushed her in and crept in after her.

They lay, panting, safe for the moment from the silent, sweeping shapes.

"What are they?" Laura panted.

"Moonbats," Sloe said.

"Moonbats!" The thought of them made her shudder again. "The Old Woman told me about them. They put out her eyelights, she told me. And killed her motherfatherfolk. Who are they after, Sloe? Us, or Spellhorn?"

"They'll snatch up anyone. One time long ago the moonbats stole a Wild One," Sloe said.

"Did they? What happened?"

"Spellhorn was sent on the seekfind. He had to go lonesome into the moonbats' cave and snatch back the Wild One. He nearly took his last forever sleep that time, all right."

"And who was the Wild One?" Laura asked.

Sloe shook his head and put his hands across his mouth. "It's not for me to give wordspeak of that," he told her. "But the Wild One came back bitter-brained, all downsad too. And the Old Woman moped about and hid herself longtime, and said she was heartsad for ever now, and something right special had been stole away, and badness come instead. And she said one day a mystery would come to make things right for us again."

Laura looked out again at the low fires. All the Wild Ones had crept away into tree holes and hiding-places under bushes. Spellhorn stood alone, his head lowered, his front foot pawing the earth. The moonbats drifted without a sound above him, casting an eerie white glow on to his back. The hornless ones moved in the shadows, circling him.

"Spellhorn! Take strength!" Sloe breathed.

But Laura closed her eyes. "If Spellhorn wins," she thought, "the Wild Ones will go on to the Wilderness, and take me with him. But if he loses, they'll have to stay for ever in these Bad Woods. And I'll be free!"

Chapter Eight

THE BATTLEBITE

SPELLHORN STOOD, WIDE-EYED and waiting. He was lit up in the night by the moonbats. He watched calmly as the hornless ones crept closer to him. He lowered his horn and it flashed, silver white.

"His spear weapon is fit to strike," Sloe whispered.

"Everything's so quiet!" Laura breathed. "I don't like it."

The silence was like a mist hissing inside her head, creeping into her ears. It seemed as if every creature in the Bad Woods was holding its breath and waiting. Nothing moved. The moonbats hung like still flames over the clearing, hovering without sound. The Wild Ones crouched in their tree caves. They were bright-eyed with watching, open-mouthed. Then little by little came a rippling as if the dark air was shivering. The moonbats dipped down their wings like oars ploughing into water, and then as if they were making waves of light they flashed in all directions, baffling and blinding. They flipped themselves over in the air and plunged like arrows of fire towards Spellhorn.

"Pierce them with your point!" Sloe yelled, leaping about on all fours in the shelter of the tree.

Laura turned her head away. "They must win!" she whispered to herself. "Or I'll never be free."

Spellhorn swung his head from side to side, stabbing at the moonbats as they flung their flapping wings at him. Their webbed talons raked his back. Their winnowing screeches scraped the air like blunt knives.

"Stab!" Sloe shouted to him.

And then, under all the beating wings and high pitched shrieks came a long, low bellowing. One by one the unicorns of darkness closed in to take their plunge. Again and again they came for Spellhorn, and again and again he dodged away from their yellow teeth and the blows of their flailing hooves. And still they came for him.

"They're biting! They're biting!" Sloe wailed. "Take eyeful, Girlchild!"

"I can't!" she said. She crouched down with her head tucked into her knees, trying to block out the swirling lights and the screeches and howls of the battlebite, and the terrible sound of ripping flesh and thudding bone.

"They're biting his back. They're beating him down. Again and more time and more," Sloe told her. His voice was quiet and whining now, whimpering like a small, frightened dog. "There'll be heart grief before the ending of this. Battle blood stains the soil."

"But they must win!" Laura couldn't help herself. She peered through her fingers at the writhing mass of beasts. She couldn't see Spellhorn. For a moment he reared up on to his hind legs, flashing his horn like a sharp sword. He tossed his head back and gazed round as if he was looking for her, and then his blue eyes glazed and closed. He staggered down and sank on to all fours. The hornless ones bellowed up to him again.

Sloe gave out a terrible wail of despair.

"His strongness seeps away like blood! He's losing life!"

Laura's father ran down the dark streets, buttoning his coat against the cold. The mists had come up from the valley, making shapes where there were none, blotting out all shadows. The stars were under cover. A few street-lights glowed and blinked.

"She must be down here somewhere," he thought. "She may have wandered into someone else's garden by mistake. But she knows the street so well. She'd soon realise she was wrong."

He stopped running when he reached the main road, knowing that Laura would never attempt to cross that on her own. There wasn't a sound to be heard; no cars, no footsteps, nothing. Suddenly there was a screech and then another; howls in the darkness. He turned round, and two fighting tomcats leapt from a wall and ran wailing down the street.

Mr Brook cupped his hands round his mouth. "Laura!" he shouted. "Laura! Come on home!"

Sloe touched Laura's arm. "They shadow up round him," he moaned. "Take eyeful how he's stumbled down. He's weak-kneed with weariness."

Laura closed her eyes.

"Our Spellhorn is fallen!" Sloe sighed. "His long forever sleep is creeping like grey duskdark upon him."

"He won't die, will he?" Laura asked.

Sloe nodded. He screwed his fists into his eyes. Laura heard a low kind of moaning around the bushes, and knew that it came from the Wild Ones, and that they were grieving for the dying unicorn. The branches across their hiding-place were pulled back and a small shape crawled in and crept up to them. It was the Old Woman. Her breath came in low hissing gasps. "Heesh!" she sighed. "Heesh!"

She put her hand to her mouth and then to Laura's ear, showing her that she wanted to speak in secret to her. Laura crouched down so her face was next to the Old Woman's.

"Give him willspeak, Girlchild."

"Me?" said Laura. "I can't help him."

The Old Woman nodded her head urgently. She looked at Spellhorn and then at Laura, and back again. Spellhorn was surrounded by the unicorns of darkness, a still white shape between their stamping legs. "See how the hornless ones throng round him," she moaned. "They've downbeaten him now, well sure. Rouse him, Girlchild. Rouse him before the too-late time. He'll live or take forever sleep for you, know that."

"For me?"

"You have the mystery power deep locked in you. Use it!"

"I don't want him to die!" Laura said slowly.

"Speak him that, then," the Old Woman urged her.

"His eye-holes grow dark with last sleep," Sloe whispered. "Do it now!"

★ ★ ★

Mrs Brook was standing on the doorstep when her husband came back up the hill.

"Is she there?" she shouted, as soon as she saw his shape looming in the mist. Then she saw that he was alone.

"Not in the street," he said quietly. He came up to her and put both his hands on her shoulders.

"And not in the garden," she said. "And not in the house. Sam's right. She's gone."

Laura pushed slowly past the Old Woman and Sloe and crawled out of the cave. Her breath made tiny gasps of fear in her throat as the hornless unicorns backed away from her and then gathered in round her again. She could smell the stink of their sweaty bodies. They growled deep in their throats and rolled their eyes at her. The earth trembled with the stamp of their hooves. Her whole body quivered as if her blood was beating in time with the earth, and the back of her neck prickled as if ice-cold ants were creeping down it.

She fixed her eyes on Spellhorn and crawled through their legs to him. She could see that his side was bleeding. She put out her hand and touched him.

"I don't want you to die," she said. "I want you to win. For me!"

The hornless unicorns reared up round her, panicking, kicking out their legs in fright. Wayfinder ran out of his shelter and hauled Laura away. He dragged her into the shadows and stood with his arms looping her so they could both watch the unicorn in safety. Spellhorn snorted and struggled to his feet. He jerked his head round, looking for Laura. His eyes were gleaming now. His legs quivered. Then he lowered his head and plunged his horn into one of his attackers. The hornless one roared and wrenched itself away. Spellhorn charged again.

"Our Spellhorn is newborn!" Wayfinder chortled.

Sloe stuck his head through the branches of his tree cave, cheering with every plunge Spellhorn took.

"He's all kick legs, all dagger head, all lightning strike!" he shouted. "Give them teeth gash, Spellhorn! Give them stab heads!"

Sloe ran out of the cave, leaping round the wounded hornless ones as they withdrew in fear and pain, to drift back like fire smoke into the heart of the Bad Woods.

"You have wounds to lick now, all right!" he shouted after them. "Hot blood for bellyfill!"

"Spellhorn has won!" cheered Wayfinder.

Sloe and his brotherfriend Fastfoot ran after the last of the hornless ones, lobbing small stones at them to make sure they kept running. Wayfinder shinned up a tree, clutching his arms and legs round it till he reached the top, and watched their retreat. The Old Woman clapped her hands in glee. One by one the Wild Ones tumbled down from branches and leapt out of tree holes, hugging and cuffing each other and hollering loudly. Some of them ran to Laura to take her hand, holding it to their wet lips, grinning at her and pulling her over to where Spellhorn was standing.

"Girlchild! He did that for you!" Water told her. "You have a Wild One's heart, all right."

Laura stroked Spellhorn's neck. He was still hot and quivering with the energy of the battlebite. "I'm so glad you won, Spellhorn," she whispered.

Flight was the last to crawl out of her hiding-place. She was shaking. Water patted her cheeks and rubbed her hands, making a low comforting hum in her throat. "All gone! All gone backhome," she told her, but Flight shrugged her away. Healhands came with some leaves to rub on Spellhorn's wounds. Laura helped her, flinching when she saw how his flesh had been torn by the teeth of the hornless unicorns.

"I should have helped you sooner," she whispered, and Spellhorn flicked his ears to show he understood. "I didn't know it would be like this, Spellhorn."

Sideman grunted when the job was done. He and Healhands inspected Spellhorn all over. "Best way speed now," he told the Old Woman. "That gang will soon get strong bones again and dash back for more."

The Old Woman heaved herself carefully on to Spellhorn's back. He turned his head to look for Laura, and she stood by him again and patted his neck.

"Throng round me, Wild Ones," the Old Woman said. "I have wordspeak for you." The Wild Ones clustered round her, some leading their horses. Sideman climbed up on to his horse, Foam, and pushed through till he was at her side. The chattering simmered down as she spoke again.

"First thing, know that I'm right heartglad to have my unicorn again time, and that he's won the battlebite for us. Now that he's with me I have eyebright again. But know this, Wild Ones. I'm still an Old Bones, and there's nothing he can do to turn that round. Now, here's the plain thing that I want to fill your ears with. When the Old Woman sleeps her last forever sleep, the Wild Ones must seekfind some new Mighty High to fill her place. Now I know why Spellhorn brought us out of the Wilderness, and what he was searching for. Deep in my mind-hole I know why. I'm telling you the new Mighty High has been found. Spellhorn has found her and brought her to us."

Laura looked round, wondering who the Old Woman could be talking about. Startled, she saw that they were all watching her, some of them with their lips drawn back over their teeth in smiles.

"She has no knowing of the Wild One ways!" protested Flight. "How can she be our Mighty High?"

"Because the unicorn is heartglad of her. That's the signal!" said Sloe.

Flight clutched the Old Woman's arm. "But I'm the oldest girlchild! I'm the one!"

The Old Woman shook her arm away. She leant down to hiss in Flight's face. "And what is precious about you, Flight? Where's it gone?"

Flight covered her face up, whimpering. The Old Woman held out her hand to Laura. "Clamber, Girlchild," she said. "My wordspeak's done."

In silence Laura climbed up behind her. The Wild Ones waited behind the Old Woman, who seemed to be deep in sad thought. At last she clicked her tongue and Spellhorn set off at a steady pace, with the Wild Ones' horses trotting behind him. They made their way without fear now through the Bad Woods. Some of them began to sing, low in their throats, a steady sheeshing croon that reminded Laura of waves swishing round rocks; a kind of lullaby. Deep inside her she felt an excitement like a flutter of snowflakes. Was she really to be the new leader of the Wild Ones?

Chapter Nine

EYE SPY HILL

AS THE DAY wore on it grew colder and colder. Laura huddled up to the Old Woman's back, wishing she had her long hair for warmth. The now-familiar rocking motion of Spellhorn's long stride comforted her, but the wind howled in a miserable, fretful way. They came out of the shelter of the Bad Woods and on to a wide, bare plain. There was no hiding-place there from the wind; it slashed at them like knives. Laura's teeth chattered and her cheeks were sore, and the ends of her fingers were pink and raw. The Wild Ones didn't seem to mind. Their horses walked on, heads down, their shaggy manes ruffling.

"Homeland soon!" Sloe shouted across to her. Excitement fizzed in the pit of Laura's stomach. Yet mixed in with it was a kind of aching for her own homeland that filled her throat and her eyes.

At last they came to a stop below some huge flat round boulders that were piled on top of each other like stone wheels or cakes of bread. Rocks and stones stood leaning against each other in all kinds of odd angles up a steep slope, making dark caves that looked like mouths wide open in surprise.

"Eye Spy Hill!" shouted Wayfinder. He slid down from his horse and stumbled up the boulders to be the first to the top. The Wild Ones tumbled down, whooping to each other, and scrambled after him. Sloe beat them all to the top. He leapt like a bony hare, with his legs bunched to spring from stone to stone. He stood at the top and pointed at something, rolled over and waved his legs in the air, and then slithered all the way down again to Laura. He grabbed her arm and began to haul her up the slope after him.

"Take eyeful, speedy before sundown," he shouted at her, his cheeks bulging with grinning.

She panted after him, grazing her hands and her knees on the scabby rocks, but laughing out loud with the Wild Ones in the excitement of the race. When she came to the top she had to battle for her breath. But the wind had dropped away.

The Wild Ones stood in silent groups, arms flung across each other's shoulders, nuzzling each other's cheeks in a kind of gentle joy. Mountains reared up to the west and east of them; mountains of ice, glittering blue-purple, with snow like a deep white shawl spreading down their lower slopes. They shone in the polish of the setting sun, taking its lick of scarlet. A pale green sea with crimson stains like blood in it lapped against the ice mountains, tinkling like shattering glass.

And on the horizon there was a break; a low stretch of land across the sea, spreading back to fold upon fold of purple hills. It shimmered, with the setting sun low and fierce behind it now; it was like a dark sequin set in the rippling silk scarf of the sea.

"Is that the Wilderness?" Laura whispered.

No sooner had she said that than the sun dipped and a pale mist like her own breath wreathed across the land and settled over it, and it disappeared from sight.

The Wild Ones sighed and rubbed their eyes as if they could make it come back again, or as if they were waking up from a deep sleep. The mist was spreading, taking the light and colour out of the sea, so it turned a sludgy brown-grey. The ice mountains lost their glitter and the wind rose up again to whine and howl like a pack of starving wolves. Some of the Wild Ones had already started to slither back down the boulders to look for shelter. Sloe nudged Laura to follow him as he ran down but Flight sidled up to her. She reminded Laura of a bird, sharp-eyed and light-footed.

"This is the last piece of menfolk before the Wilderness, Girlchild," Flight told her. "Think again about backhome."

Laura stared at her. Back home? How could she go home now?

"Take eyeful," Flight said. "Now that the moon's white eye is open wide."

Laura turned back and looked across the sea. It heaved and tumbled now with the wind's roughness, as if it was rolling with dark beasts. And as she looked, she saw that there *were* beasts, that far below her on the shoreline long dark shapes wriggled and slithered down into the foam.

"What are they?" she asked.

The Old Woman and Water had joined them now. They stood gazing down at the seething waves. "This is the Sea of Snakes," the Old Woman said.

"The Wild Ones must cross it to reach the Wilderness," Flight said. "Only the true Wild Ones can do that thing."

"But how?" asked Laura. "How could anyone go in there? I'm not! I'm *not*."

"No other way," Flight laughed.

"Can't we go over the mountains?"

"Too far," the Old Woman shook her head. "Our Spellhorn could go that way, but not our horses. Their hooves would spin on all that ice shine."

"Day come day go the snakes and worms slither down to this sea. They spit their poison there," Flight told Laura.

"Poison?"

Flight laughed again. "And you must fishyswim in it, all waggle arms and kick legs, like the rest."

"I'm never going in there," Laura called after her, as like a brown sea-bird Flight skimmed away down the slope, spreading her arms wide to steady herself with each leap.

The Old Woman clucked. "Flight, where's your heart warmth gone?" she sighed. She patted Laura's arm. "The Wild Ones can cross the snake sea," she assured her. "But menfolk can't, that's for sure." She crouched so she could make her way back down on all fours, loping sideways and clinging on to cracks in the stones with her long nails.

"Don't be heartsad," Water said to Laura. "If Spellhorn has longings to take you to the Wilderness, you'll come." She shivered, hugging herself against the cold. "Now dash down, Girlchild. This wind has biting teeth. Scuttle down to cave dens before it nips off your hear-hole flaps."

Laura took a last look at the snake sea. It was seething now with heads that bobbed and gleamed in the moonlight. She ran after Water and the Old Woman, kicking small stones as she went, sending them scuttering down into the valley where the horses munched thin grass. She crawled into one of the mouth caves, glad to get out of the shrill of the wind. She snuggled in between Flight and Sloe, and lay listening to the grunts and squeaks they made in their sleep. And she could hear voices, whispering in her head.

Sam had a phone call from his dad to say they would soon be moving back into their own house.

"When?" Sam shouted, excited. He hated being at Laura's house now. Her parents watched out for her, sad and quiet, telling each other that she would come back, but Sam knew that deep in their hearts they thought that they would never see their daughter again.

"Soon, Sam," his dad promised. "We'll be able to get to work on the house any day now. Why don't you go down and have a look at it. You might like to choose a new colour for the front door…"

Sam wheeled his bike out of Mr Brook's garage for the first time since the night of the wild horses. He paused for a moment, gazing up at the hill slope with its scattering of grey humped boulders on the skyline, and remembered Laura making her way up there with Queenie.

"I wish I could do something to help you, Laura," he whispered. He heard the bunched crows cackling in the trees around him, and shuddered. He swung himself up on to his bike and drove the pedals hard till he was freewheeling down the hill to the village.

In the houses in the main street people were busy painting the blackened walls and putting up new wallpaper. After all, not a great deal of damage had been done. No one had been badly hurt, though they'd been very shocked. The alarms had been raised so quickly that the fires had soon been put out. People were still mystified as to the cause of it, though. Fire chiefs were inspecting all the electric wiring, and scientists were taking samples of the building materials for testing. Sam's house still stood empty, but his next-door neighbour, old Mrs Grey, was outside her own house touching up her front door with green paint.

"You'll have a bit of fun, Sam, helping with the decorating," she told him.

"It's Mum and Dad who'll have the fun," he grumbled. "They'll probably have me cleaning up and making tea, knowing them."

"Never mind," she said. "It'll be nice to have you all back home again, and things back to normal." She turned to go back in.

"Mrs Grey," Sam said, "can I ask you something?"

She turned, her brush upright in her hand and paint dripping down its handle.

"It's about unicorns."

"Unicorns!" Mrs Grey laughed. "Why d'you want to ask me about unicorns, Sam?"

"Because I think Laura's been kidnapped by one."

"Laura? Haven't they found her yet?" Mrs Grey sighed. "I heard she'd gone missing. As if this village hasn't had enough trouble already."

"I saw her on a unicorn's back," Sam said firmly. She looked at him and smiled. "Mrs Grey, I think I did."

He followed her down her hall and into the kitchen. She put her paint brush into a jar of white spirit and squeezed washing-up liquid on to her hands. Then she rinsed them under the tap again and again till all the soapy bubbles had floated away. She dried her hands slowly on the towel, deep in thought.

"Tell me more about this, Sammy," she said. She led him into her back room. It was untouched by the fire, and was filled now with early morning sunshine and the rich spicy smell of carnations.

"It came to Laura's garden a few times during the

fires," Sam said. "But I didn't see it till it took Laura away."

Mrs Grey knelt down on the floor by her book case. Sam knelt next to her.

"Unicorns are mythical creatures," she told him. "Fabulous beasts that people believed in thousands of years ago, and through time. They're even mentioned in the Bible."

"So they really do exist," Sam said.

Mrs Grey smiled. "It would be wonderful to think they do, Sam. They seem to belong to a better time, a simpler time, that we all have a yearning to go back to. Do you understand what I mean?"

Sam nodded. "I think I do."

"But there's no real proof of them. Here. Read this." She found the book she was looking for and opened it out on the rug. There was an illustration of a white creature like a horse, with a long, creamy mane and little beard, and a slender pearly horn between its ears.

"Yes," Sam breathed. "That was it."

Mrs Grey looked sideways at him. "I don't like to think of it taking children away, Sam."

"She said she could see it. Not just in her mind's eye. She really saw it."

Mrs Grey sat back on her heels. "Did she? Did she? She must have wanted it then, very, very much."

"Mrs Grey," said Sam slowly. "D'you know if it's possible to capture a unicorn?"

The old lady was bending forwards again to look at the book. Wisps of grey hair trickled across her face and she brushed them away. "It was hunted for its horn," she said. "And some people claim to have captured it. By trickery, Sam. Read it."

"The unicorn's horn, or alicorn," read Sam, "was valuable as a cure against a range of illnesses. Nearly two and a half thousand years ago Greek physicians claimed to use it as a cure for poison. It was hunted throughout the world for its magical horn, but could never be captured by force." He looked up at Mrs Grey, his eyes shining. "But there is a way…"

"Go on," she nodded. "Read on."

"One day a man called John of Hesse saw a unicorn come down to a river. As it was standing there, snakes and serpents came down to the river to shed their poison in it, so that no animals could drink there. The unicorn stepped forward and dipped its horn into the water, and instantly it was pure again, and the other animals gathered round to drink their fill…"

"Any more?"

"… A unicorn can never be taken by force. But it was said that it would come willingly to a young girl…"

★   ★   ★

Laura sat up suddenly, listening. She could hear the yelping of the wind, and the roar of the sea, and the snuffling of the sleeping Wild Ones. And over all this, she could hear the sound of voices, calling her.

"Girl! Girl! Come out."

On all fours she crawled out of the boulder mouth. There were no stars. Dense clouds hugged the moon. There was nothing to be seen out there, nothing, except for the pale huddle of sleeping horses down in the valley. Spellhorn stood apart from them, a white ghost beast in the swimming dark. Surely it wasn't his voice she'd heard?

"Girl!"

"Who is it?"

"Sh! We've come to save you."

"Come to take you home."

So there were two voices, zizzing backwards and forwards like wasps.

"But who are you? You're not Wild Ones!"

The voices buzzed with suppressed laughter.

"Wild Ones! I should say we're not."

"We're your friends, girl, that's us."

"Come to take you home."

"That's it. To your mum and dad. And your dog. Want to go home?"

Laura put out her hands to try and touch the voices,

but they were out of reach, swimming round her. "Of course I do."

"Just one thing," a voice said.

"One thing first."

"We want a trophy. See that unicorn."

Spellhorn tossed back his head, whinnying softly.

"We want his horn!" The first voice came again.

"His magic horn!" the second voice buzzed. "And then we'll take you home."

"But he'd never let you take it from him," Laura said. "He'd spear you through with it."

"Oh, we're not going to touch him." The voices danced round her head, first one, then the other, breaking in on each other and sometimes both speaking at once. "No one can capture a unicorn. We know that. Men have been trying to capture unicorns since the world began."

"Then how are you going to get his horn?" Laura asked.

"You are!" The voices laughed like bells. "You are!"

"But how?"

"He comes readily to you."

"We've seen you talking to him."

"He's like a lamb when you're near him."

"Sit by him and sing to him."

"And when he kneels by you and puts his head in your lap…"

"Snatch his horn and snap it off!"

While the voices were speaking Laura had found herself being drawn down, down, almost without knowing it, till she was standing near Spellhorn. The last voice made her stop.

"No!" she shouted.

The voices were soft and gentle again now, wheedling, coaxing. "Oh, it won't hurt him," they said.

"Won't hurt him a bit. It's easy."

"Then you run to us with it and we'll get you home."

"I can't do it," she said.

"Go on, girl. Do it now. While this lot's asleep."

She hesitated. If it was that easy... if it wouldn't hurt him... "But he's watching me."

"He'll come to you when you sing to him, you know he will."

"Do it!"

The strange thing was, when Spellhorn lifted up his head and looked at Laura, it was almost as if he was willing her to go to him. She went forward very slowly, and began to hum, soft in her throat, the tune she'd heard Water sing to the Wild Ones.

"Good girl," whispered the first voice. "Take it steady. Take it slow." "Come to me, Spellhorn," Laura whispered. "Come and kneel by me."

She sat down on the grass and the unicorn stepped slowly over to her.

"Let me stroke you," she said. Spellhorn knelt down next to her. She was shaking.

"Now!" the voices breathed.

"Lay your head down, Spellhorn. Let me stroke you."

Laura. A sound like silver flutes seemed to come from Spellhorn himself. *Would you betray me?*

She shook her head. Tears were welling up in her eyes.

"Now!" the hissing voices said.

Laura, would you betray me?

"No, Spellhorn, no!" Laura sobbed. "I only want to stroke you."

"Now, girl. Now. Now. Now."

And the fluty voice came from Spellhorn again, soft and sad. *Laura. Would you betray me?*

Laura jumped up. She pushed the unicorn away from her.

"No!" she shouted to the voices. "I won't do it. I won't."

At that moment Spellhorn reared up on to his hind legs and lashed out. The horses charged, screaming and neighing. The Wild Ones ran shouting out of the caves. In the terrible roaring darkness Laura knew that the voices had fled for ever. She stood in the middle of the clamour and put her arms round Spellhorn's neck, trying to calm him, and trying to tell him she was sorry. The Old Woman came up to her and put her hand on her shoulder.

"Did you hear them?" Laura asked. She kept her head buried against Spellhorn.

"We all did. We had our eyes wide to eye spy you, too."

"I'm sorry," Laura sobbed.

"But you didn't do it, and that's the special thing, Girlchild. You've passed the hardest test of all time." The Old Woman looked down at Flight, who was crouched on the ground by Spellhorn, her head tucked down into her arms. She put the ball of her foot on Flight's knee and tipped her backwards, making her curl up into a roll of misery.

"You're one of the Wild Ones now, for ever sure," she told Laura. "There'll be no go-back time now. Come dawnlight sun-up you'll be in the Wilderness. Your home!"

Chapter Ten

INTO THE SEA OF SNAKES

IT WAS WATER and Wayfinder who took Laura down to
the sea's edge next morning. The Wild Ones came behind
them, coaxing the horses over the crest of Eye Spy Hill.
Sideman and Horseman shuffled from one horse to
another and fussed round them like anxious sheepdogs,
growling if they thought they were being put in any
danger. The horses were nervous of the loose rocks; they
rolled their eyes and pricked back their ears in fright.

Spellhorn came lightly and easily, and the Old Woman panted after him.

Pebbles scrunched under Laura's feet as she came down from the boulders of the hill. Soon the pebbles gave way to coarse, gritty sand that her heels sank into. Here and there she could see the smooth curving tracks the snakes had made as they'd writhed down to the sea. The waves came in with a sigh and trickled back again; shoosh, kheeeh, shoosh, kheeeh; and through that gentle sound she could hear the hissing of snakes. Now in the gleaming backs of the waves she could see them, their speckled browns and yellows and greens, the amber stare of their eyes, the flicker of their tongues. She shivered. Water blew on her cheeks, trying to warm her.

"I'm not cold," Laura told her. "I'm scared stiff."

The Old Woman chuckled as she came to join them. Spellhorn stared at the sea and snorted. It was some sort of comfort, anyway, to have him near. One by one the other Wild Ones appeared. Their horses shied back from the creeping foam, seeing the snakes tumbling there. Nobody said anything. They just looked at the long stretch of sea between land and the misty horizon, and scratched their chins, and sighed.

"Not longtime," the Old Woman promised.

Then they started to edge away, without a sound, and Laura found that she was standing alone with Spellhorn.

She could hear the mumble of voices as the Wild Ones crowded up against the boulders to watch her.

"The girlchild has heart fear to do the job," said Water.

"It must be done, all same," the Old Woman said. There were grunts of agreement.

"My brainbox says she'll tumble in and shrivel up," Flight giggled.

"Keep gob shut," Sloe warned her. "Or I'll pummel you."

"Her skin coat will float away from her bones, most like," Sideman said.

"Spellhorn should be full of spite with her," Flight pouted. "He nearly lost the battlebite. He nearly had his horn stole off."

Still Laura stood, unable to move, while Spellhorn watched her.

"Maybe his strongness is all drained off," Wayfinder said. "Maybe his power's long lost."

Laura couldn't stop trembling. She couldn't run back to join the others. She couldn't bring herself to step forward to where the snakes raised their gleaming heads. She imagined them wrapping their slimy bodies round her legs, or slithering up her arms. She imagined treading on one.

Spellhorn waited.

"It's the now time, Girlchild," the Wild Ones started to shout at her. "Get done."

"Trust the unicorn!" Sloe shouted. "Speak heartsoft to him."

"And easyfoot now," Water warned. "There won't be another chance."

Laura took a deep breath and put her hand on Spellhorn's neck. He stood steady while she talked to him.

"Spellhorn. I'm sorry about the battlebite. I'm sorry I nearly gave your horn away. I'll never, never do anything like that again."

He tossed his head back, snorting.

"He gives her shakehead. All's lost!" Sideman groaned.

"Hush, Blabmouth," the Old Woman hissed. "Take earful."

Laura stroked Spellhorn's nose. "Think of the Wild Ones," she whispered. "Only you can lead them to the Wilderness."

The Old Woman grunted and nodded round to Flight and Sideman. "That's the speak!" she grinned.

"I trust you to take me through the poison water, Spellhorn," Laura said. "I'll come in with you." She clambered up on to his back. He squared himself, ready. "I trust you, Spellhorn."

"He'll no time do it," Flight breathed.

The unicorn stepped forward. He stopped his hooves at the very edge of the dry sand. Then he slowly lowered his head. Laura lurched forward and clung on to his mane, thinking that Flight was right and that he was going to toss her into the sea. The snakes hissed and bobbed, and reared their heads again.

"I trust you, Spellhorn!" But her voice was small in her throat.

Spellhorn lowered his horn right down till the tip was in the water. The sea boiled, gushing up a hiss of steam. The snakes reared up, lashing out again and again with their tongues, spitting, leaping. Spellhorn dipped his horn again, and this time there was a clanging in the sea, like the chiming of hundreds of iron bells, a deep booming that seemed to echo under the ocean. One by one the snakes curled away from him. They lowered their heads and swam out in a wide half-circle away from him, and the sun caught the dazzle of their flashing brilliance. They slid up on to the beach and the rocks at the far end of the shore, and they were the colours of jewels, amethyst and emerald and topaz, glittering in coils.

The sea cleared to blue, and the sandbed underneath it gleamed like ripples of gold.

"The sea's bright clear!" Sloe shouted.

"And sweet as summer rain!" laughed Water.

The Wild Ones surged forward, splashing and cheering. They dived in and thrashed their arms and legs in it, ducked each other's heads under it, shook themselves like dogs, put their mouths in it and tried to drink it dry.

"Get on, guzzlemouths," the Old Woman told them, though she was laughing too and splashing Sideman with her kicks of joy. "No time now before the snakes slide back."

Laura made room for her on Spellhorn, and he leaned forward into the gentle waves until they lifted him up and he began to float. The horses swam in a long line, holding their heads up high. From time to time Sloe and two of his brotherfriends, Fastfoot and Woodfetch, dived off their horses' backs and dog-paddled round them, laughing and bubbling as they ducked their heads down, twisting round on to their backs and lazing and bobbing in the sunshine. They all seemed to take their strength from Spellhorn, and he floated with no effort at all, calm as a white swan, drifting in a circle round them all while the Wild Ones sang out loud and the Old Woman urged them on.

And on the far shore, one by one, the snakes uncoiled themselves and slithered back down into the sea.

Suddenly a howl broke through the Wild Ones' singing. Spellhorn stopped and trod water while Laura and the Old Woman twisted themselves round on his back to scan the sea.

"Give help to me! Give help hand!"

The cry came from under the water. One of the Wild Ones was floundering way back behind them all.

"Help hand!"

A shape surfaced, its hair spread out like seaweed, in a blood-red swirl of cloak.

"It's Flight!" said Laura. "She's fallen in!"

"She's tried to fishyswim, more like," tutted the Old Woman. "And lost her strongness. Well," – she turned her head away – "let her sink."

"No!" gasped Laura. "We can't do that. We'll have to save her." She tried to urge Spellhorn to turn his head round so he could float over to where Flight bobbed up and down in the water.

"Too-late time," the Old Woman said. "No turn-back time for us. Take eyeful there."

Laura could see the silvery gleam of the snakes leaping through the waves towards them.

"They're flicking fast," the Old Woman said. "No time."

"But Spellhorn can clear the water for us again." Laura tried desperately to kick him round. Flight held her arms out to them. She went under. The Old Woman wrenched Spellhorn's head towards the line of swimming horses heading for home.

"I tell you, too-late time! His power's all sizzled down. You heard the water sing with it! He needs long shuteye time to bring it back again."

"But Flight!" Laura moaned.

She looked back over her shoulder. Flight was growing weaker.

"Give me help hand!"

The Old Woman snapped her teeth together. "She had the know-how to save herself one time long ago. And she lost it, chucked it out. Leave her, Girlchild. She's a no good now."

She kicked Spellhorn on, and as she did so Laura slipped down from his back and slid into the water. She had no idea where she found the strength to swim to Flight, or how she managed to put her arms round her neck and heave her up so she could swim back with her, kicking her feet like flippers. The Wild Girl was like a dead weight, but she struggled in her fright, and Laura found herself going under with her. They came up at last against Spellhorn's side, weak and gasping. The unicorn gave a light whinny. The Old Woman looked down in surprise.

"So," she tutted. "So so so." She leaned down and heaved Flight up, so the Wild Girl lay across Spellhorn's back with her arms and legs dangling down into the water.

"No room for both," she told Laura. "Hold fast, Girlchild."

But Laura felt as if all her strength was draining away, like the water that was streaming from Flight's long hair.

She could hardly lift her arms to swim. She could hardly move her feet to paddle.

"The snakes have swallowed up the space we left behind," the Old Woman shouted. "Hold fast. Hold fast."

Spellhorn drove his feet down so the water churned up behind him. Laura's hands grasped out for his mane, and slipped away. She clutched up again and found Flight's arms and clung to them. Slowly her fingers started sliding down. She closed her hands in Flight's, grasping on to them, but gradually the Wild Girl's fingers opened out. For a second their fingertips touched. Then Laura slid away, and found herself being sucked down, down, into the swirl of the sea.

Chapter Eleven

THE WILDERNESS

LAURA WAS AWAKENED by the sound of gentle waves shushing through sand. Something wet dabbed at her cheek. She opened her eyes to find that she was lying on a beach and that Spellhorn was nuzzling her with his damp nose. The Wild Ones were crouched in an anxious ring round her. They chuckled to themselves and cuffed each other softly as she looked round at them. The Old Woman clapped her fists together over her head.

"The worry time is over," she told them all. "Let the girlchild gasp for breath."

Laura sat up and the Wild Ones crept back, widening the circle round her. The soft sands she was lying in were speckled with the colours of crushed shells – salmon pink and peach, early sky blue, lemon, cream. Further up the shore the shells were whole and perfect. Small Wild Children were playing there, and Wild Women that Laura had never seen before clung to each other in a gossiping line, hugging tiny long-haired babies to themselves and staring at her.

"Take life sip, now the tide and Spellhorn have fetched you home to us," said Water, holding out a shell to Laura's lips. It was brimming with a golden liquid that tasted of many different fruits crushed together, cool and sweet. Laura drank it down and stood up, feeling strong again.

"Now Sloe can show you the Wilderness, all round," Water laughed.

Laura ran after Sloe, scrunching her feet through the sand. They soon left the beach and came to a copse of tall spindly trees, and wild flowers that twisted up above their heads like coloured stars and drenched the air with perfume. The silky leaves and petals tickled Laura's skin as she ran, twisting and wisping round her bare arms and legs. Freckles of light sparkled on the velvety ground.

Wherever they went, groups of Wild Ones were busy

collecting wood to make or mend their shelters. Little Wild Ones ran backwards and forwards, cradling armloads of twigs, while their motherfatherfolk staggered along with heavy branches, or rolled logs. They stopped to stare at Laura, sometimes holding up their fists to say hello or pulling their lips back over their teeth in wide grins. They chattered to each other after she'd gone, or shinned up trees to keep sight of her.

But soon Laura and Sloe had left the busy places behind. They had come to the quiet heart of the Wilderness. They were away from the shelter of trees and high plants, so they'd lost the piping of birds. In front of them were the humps of hills, and they were as huge and as quiet as slumbering beasts.

"Let's take the long dash up!" Sloe said. He scampered away ahead of Laura up the bluey slopes.

"Wait for me!" she shouted.

But he was anxious to get to the top. He stopped now and again to wait for her, but as soon as she caught up with him he was off again, leaving her breathless and cross. When she reached the top she flung herself down next to him, gasping.

"Take eyeful now!" he urged her. "Look at all the Wilderness lights."

She stood up at last and looked round her. The Wilderness was blazing with colours.

"All dazzle, all places," said Sloe happily. "And all its rushdowns. Look!"

He pointed at a waterfall that splashed down the slope and seemed to wind round and round in the blue of rivers till it reached the far, tiny shelters of the Wild Ones.

"Behind that rushdown there's my special place," he told her. "It's the secret eye of the Wilderness. Find it, Girlchild!"

Sloe leapt ahead of her. Laura turned slowly round on the hilltop, so all the colours of the Wilderness swam like a rainbow sea round her. Somewhere out there was manfolk land. She couldn't see it. She turned slowly round again, trying to see into the misty horizon, far beyond the colour sparkle.

Then she raced down the hill after Sloe.

The waterfall sprayed a cold drizzle on her cheeks and arms as she ran to it. She stood by it with her eyes closed and her mouth wide open, drinking it in.

Sloe jumped down at her like a wild cat.

"It's all right for you, Wild One Sloe," she said, startled. "You know this place and all its hiding-holes. I don't."

"Soon will," he told her. "Your home now. Here." He pulled back a curtain of trailing moss and ferns that dripped waterdrops. "Here's the secret eye."

Laura followed him into the dark and echoey depths of the cave. Its walls glowed with colour. When she crawled further, and her eyes got used to the darkness, she realised that the coloured daubs were paintings of birds and animals and plants. "Who's done these, Sloe?" she asked. "You?"

He nodded, grinning, and ran outside again to search the ground for something. He lifted up the fern strands and rolled some small coloured pebbles across to her, then crawled in again carrying a large flat stone. He rubbed one of the pebbles on it till it crumbled into a fine red dust, which he scooped into the cupped palm of his hand. Then he spat into it and mixed it round with his finger to make a paste, and used his finger to daub the cave wall with it. He hunkered down with his feet flat on the ground and his chin on his knees and swayed backwards and forwards and from side to side as he worked, snoring slightly with concentration. Laura sat on her feet and watched him. First he drew the outline of a large bird with outspread, ragged wings, and filled it in with the red amber. Then he crumbled a purple-blue stone to dust and made a paste in his other palm, and used it to darken the wing tips and to paint in long, trailing tail-feathers. Then he painted in the eyes, sand-yellow.

"What's that?" asked Laura.

"He's our warrior-worrier," said Sloe. "He safekeeps the Wild Ones if danger times are near. He's the first of the earth birds. He lives in high trees and hilltops, never seen. But when he drifts down, then sad times come, right sure."

"Sad times?" said Laura. "What sort of sad times?"

Sloe hunched his shoulders up and grunted. He pushed the pebbles across to Laura. "Do word-pictures," he said.

Laura picked out a white pebble. It was round and smooth; she liked the feel of it. She scrubbed it on the flat stone to make the powder, and spat on it, as Sloe had done. But she found it hard to spread it on the bumpy cave wall with her fingers. She went outside and broke a twig off one of the feather trees, and used it as a brush. At first she didn't know what she was painting, but it grew into an animal body.

"Spellhorn!" Sloe laughed at her effort. "That's a makesmile one, that is!"

But it wasn't Spellhorn. It was squatter, with a smaller head and shorter legs. Laura couldn't remember what it was called. She wasn't sure whether she'd ever actually seen an animal like it, but somewhere in her memory she could smell it, warm and damp, and as she touched up the outline of the body with paste from a mustard yellow stone she could almost feel the animal, soft-haired, and the lick of its wet tongue on her hands.

"Not Spellhorn," she told Sloe. "Another creature, far away. With a deep growly voice like Sideman." They both laughed at that. Sloe bunched his hand up and held it towards her, and she did the same to him, so their fists touched lightly, in the way the Wild Ones did to share jokes.

Then Sloe crumbled some more stones to a paste, and painted a small twig dangling with purple berries. "My picture name," he said.

"Sloe!" said Laura. "You're a berry sloe! I thought your name meant slow – not fast!"

He pouted, drooping his shoulders down.

"But you are fast!" she told him. "I've seen you running with Fastfoot. You're as good as him any day."

He bulged his cheeks out, proud now. "Now your picture name," he said.

Laura looked at the stones. She had no idea what colour to choose for her name. She rolled the pebbles round and in the end she chose the brightest one, the colour that had surprised her the most when she'd seen her first flowers: yellow. "I don't know how to draw 'Laura'," she said. "Laura Brook." She said her name slowly. It sounded strange now. She puzzled in her head, nagging at an idea that wouldn't come out. She knew what her letters were but she didn't know their shape.

Spellhorn was outside; she heard him whinnying. She

went outside and stood stroking him while she thought about how to draw her name for Sloe. Her fingers touched the sharp tip of his horn.

"I know how!" she shouted. She ran and found a broad, flat leaf that was quite dry and papery, and then broke a sharp thorn from a branch. Sloe squatted next to her as she pierced some holes in the leaf. She closed her eyes and ran her fingers over the raised holes. Sloe did the same. "My name!" she said, but he was puzzled. Then she crawled back into the cave and pressed the leaf against the wall. She dipped her finger into her yellow paste and rubbed it through the holes, then carefully peeled away the leaf. And there was her picture name. Laura Brook.

It would glow there forever, like freckles of sunlight, in the dark eye of the Wilderness.

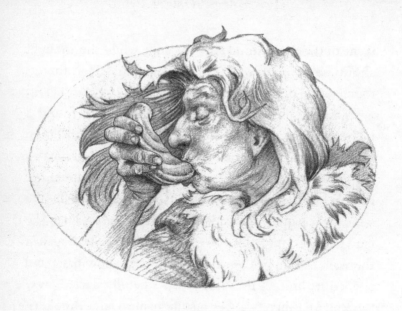

Chapter Twelve

THE WELCOME HOME BELLYFILL

WHEN THEY CAME out again into the sunlight they could hear a hollow drumming, like the beating of a heart. Spellhorn stood with his ears pricked back, listening to the sound. Laura stroked him.

"What is it, Spellhorn?" she asked.

The drumming turned to a shrill piping, an urgent sound that hovered in the air and seemed to shred it. Sloe cupped his hands to his ears and turned his head, trying to catch the direction of it.

"What's happening?" Laura asked him.

"The earth beast has been found," he said. "Dash down and watch the pounce."

Laura kicked Spellhorn on and Sloe loped after them, following the bright sound of the reed pipe. After a while Spellhorn slowed down and Sloe dodged along the path in front of them. He put his palms to the earth and began to creep. The pink soles of his feet rose and fell like little mouths opening and shutting. He stopped and turned round, putting his hands over his mouth to tell Laura to keep quiet, and she slid down off Spellhorn's back and crouched after him, head down. In front of them some Wild Ones were bunched together on all fours, watching something. Sloe and Laura crawled up to them. Now they could see that Wild Ones were spread out all round them making a big silent ring, and in the middle of it was a beast of some sort. It stood with its feet planted slightly apart, its head lowered and its heavy sides swaying.

"The earth beast!" whispered Sloe.

"What's it doing?" Laura asked.

The Wild Ones near her put their hands over their mouths and hissed at her to be quiet.

The wailing of the reed pipe soared higher and higher. There was a zizzing of insects round their heads, and blue flashes from their tiny throbbing wings. Sideman stood up slowly. He held up a sharpened spear.

"No," said Laura. "Don't kill it!"

Wild Ones stood up all round her and moved slowly in, not walking forward but swaying from side to side, knees bent, arms spread wide, in a kind of dream dance. The earth beast stood solid and blinking, staring solemnly from one to the other and lifting its legs from time to time in a kind of swaying dance of its own, echoing theirs with its own heavy grace. From round the circle voices chanted softly.

"Welcome, earth beast. Give earful to our many thanks."

"We will take bellyfill of your strongnesses."

"We will learn all your wild ways."

"If you give yourself to the Wild Ones, the Wild Ones will give shelter to your young."

"Your flesh will make our flesh firm."

"Your blood will be bright in our bodies."

"We will give back to the earth what we have snatched up."

"We live with the earth beasts and we are the earth beasts, same thing."

The Wild Ones waited, then parted a way so the beast could run if it chose to. It stayed. With one clean thrust Sideman speared it. The Wild Ones gathered round it as it sank down.

"Is it dead now?" Laura asked.

Sloe nodded. "Only that one. Wild Ones take what they need from the earth, no more. Earth beasts come to us when we need them. That's all."

"But how could you kill it?"

Sloe looked puzzled. He screwed up his face and scratched his head with his long nails, then spread out the big pink palms of his hands as if the question was too huge to be answered.

"We live with the earth beasts and we are the earth beasts, same thing," he shrugged. He scampered away from her to help the beast bearers and grubwomen at their task, and Laura went slowly back to Spellhorn.

A young Wild Girl was waiting for her there. She held her fist out to Laura and smiled. Laura put out her fist to her.

"My given name is Fern," said the Wild Girl. "I'm your sisterfriend."

"I'm Laura."

"Girlchild." Fern smiled. "That's a better given name."

"All right. Girlchild. But I wish I had a proper Wild One name."

"What like?" Fern asked.

"Daylight," said Laura.

Fern doubled over with laughter. "Daylight! That's an allwrong name for you, Girlchild. You're a midnight girl, know that. All mystery!" She ran away from Laura, still laughing. "Berry-gather wants some help. Dash down with me!"

Laura stood where she was, gazing after Fern. *Midnight*. The name chimed like a bell out of her far past. It came from a long ago time of shadowlight.

Sloe found Laura and Fern much later, their mouths and hands stained red with berries, and their leaf baskets full.

"It's time for the welcome home bellyfill," he called to them, licking his lips. They picked up their baskets and ran with him to the eating place. Already the fires had been lit, and as they ran towards them they could hear a kind of steady drumming that seemed to make the earth dance.

The Wild Ones were sitting in groups round the big feast that had been prepared for them. The women sat on one side, their babies clinging to them; then the girls. Laura and Fern went to sit by Flight and the only other Wild Girl Laura knew yet, Ash. Sloe ran to sit with Fastfoot. The men were drumming with the flats of their palms on the ground, and as soon as they were sure that everyone was there the boys joined in, putting in a much faster beat with the ends of their fingers. The rhythm grew faster and faster, and the drummers bent and swayed, nodding their heads and tossing back their long hair. A Wild Woman called Grass stood up and began to sway, bending and twisting her arms over her head as if they were snakes, and she was joined by another and another, till they looked like fields of tall grasses with the wind rippling through them.

The tapping grew to a loud crescendo, like the thundering of rain, and the dancing grew more and more frenzied. All the women and girls were joining in. Then there was a shout from the Old Woman, and the beating stopped, like gentle rain, fading, fading, and the dancers sank back slowly to their places, like leaves drifting to the ground.

"Give your word-thanks to the Wilderness," the Old Woman sang into the silence, and Water stood up. As she sang each line it was echoed first by the women, then by the girls, then the boys, then the men, in a pattern of voices that crossed and lapped each other till the words were lost in a swirl of sounds.

"How it shifts and shimmers in sequin shades," she began, and as the girls took those words up she carried on.

"How it has flashes of fishes

And smoulderings of smoke

How it is rainbowed in dewlight

How ice-blue, sun-gold, day-white…" and the words seemed to flicker as the different voices came and went… "sequin… fishes… smoke… rain… ice… flash…"

When the last voice had died away the Old Woman stood up. She was tired and weak, but she reached down for her shell of amber liquid and held it up high towards the sun. Then she tilted back her head and tipped the juice into her open mouth, allowing it to splash over her face and trickle down her chin and her neck. All the Wild Ones raised theirs to the sun, catching its colour and its warmth, and then poured it over their mouths. They laughed and shouted, smacking their lips and licking their chins, lapping up the last drops as if this was the first drink they had ever had.

They tossed their empty shells away and knelt down to grab out for the food, and for a time all chattering stopped as they grunted and chewed. Laura noticed that the Old Woman had crawled away to one side and was lying on her belly with her knees tucked under her and her chin resting on her folded arms, just humming to herself, watching the Wild Ones feasting. Spellhorn knelt by her and she reached an arm across to fondle his neck. Laura scooped some food up in her hands, like the Wild Ones, and carried it over to the Old Woman. She sniffed and shook her head. She seemed very drowsy.

"So," she said. "And are you heartglad to be here, Girlchild?"

Laura nodded. She couldn't begin to find the words to tell the Old Woman how she felt about the Wilderness.

"It's a forever place," she tried, in the language of the Wild Ones. "Alltime peace. I have heart's ease here."

The Old Woman grunted, pleased. "My heart is easy now, all right," she said. "I've brought the Wild Ones safekeep home. That's the main job done." She yawned widely, lapping her lips with her tongue, like a cat. "But I'm right wearybones. I'll crawl to my skin hut now."

Spellhorn stirred at her side, and she chuckled. "No, beast friend," she said. "Old Bones hasn't got the strongness left to clamber on your back." She pulled herself up on to her hands and knees. "Come and have wisewords with me when the stars shine out, Girlchild. And then I can shut eyes for my last earth sleep."

She started to crawl away.

"I don't know what you mean, Old Woman."

The Old Woman turned. Laura could see the pale glint of her eyes through the swing of her long white hair. "I think in your mind-hole you'll know the why-why," she said.

Laura watched her as she picked her way on her hands and knees towards the low skin tents slung under the trees. The Wild Ones, scooping up their food by the fistful and sucking it out of their palms, didn't seem to notice.

Laura couldn't eat anything now. She watched the evening light grow to dusky purple, and the sun like crimson fire slip down behind the trees. The Wild Ones, full and belching, made their drowsy way to their skin huts to sleep off their journey and their good feast. Some of them had lit smaller fires and sat round them, humming sleepily and whistling through their bared teeth, the sound the wind makes through sharp grass.

The stars came like flowers, opening out in the navy-blue field of the sky. They glowed huge and brilliant, white and blood-red and green-blue. They glimmered and swooped and spun; a kind of dance of fireworks. Laura lay on her back, staring up at them as they flickered like a swarm of brilliant insects.

Then a large, dark shape loomed across them, with a slow and steady whooshing of huge wings. It circled overhead, hovering over the quiet camp. In the light of the stars and the firelight Laura could see its scarlet, tattered wings, its long blue tail feathers, its amber eyes…

"It's the warrior-worrier," she thought. "Safekeeping the Wild Ones."

The bird fanned out its wings and began to glide down towards the camp. It drifted round the silent ring of skins as if it was a bird of prey quartering a field, and then it came to rest on the tree above the Old Woman's shelter. It dropped its tattered wings down and let the tail feathers flutter softly, so it looked like a ragged banner, or a flag drawn to half-mast.

Laura heard again the words Sloe had spoken in the cave.

"And when he drifts down, sad times come, right sure."

Chapter Thirteen

THE PASSING OF THE MIGHTY HIGH

THE OLD WOMAN'S tent was made of animal skins, stretched across branch poles. The floor was strewn with soft leaves and ferns that smelt sharp and sweet. Laura crawled across them and crouched next to the sleeping Old Woman. She was curled up under an animal fur, her fists tucked under her chin. She reminded Laura of that strange thing that Sloe had said at the slaying of the earth beast: "We live with the earth beasts and we are the earth beasts, same thing."

The Old Woman's eyes flickered open. She reached out a fluttering hand to draw Laura closer to her.

"I like this tent," Laura said to her. "It smells of forests and horses."

"And come day sun-up it will be yours to live in," the Old Woman told her. "When they've wrapped me up in flowers for my last forever sleep."

Laura shuddered, but the Old Woman's hand was warm and comforting.

"Girlchild," she said. "Soon you will take on the Mighty High of the Wild Ones. There's no heart heaviness in this, know that."

Laura nodded, but her throat was dry and sore. The Old Woman's voice had grown so weak it was almost a whimper. Laura had to lean forward to hear her.

"Of all the Wild Womenfolk, love best the one called Water. She's the warm-heart one. She'll keep you glad."

"I know, Old Woman."

"And look to Wayfinder for your safekeep."

"I will."

"And there's great heart friendship for you in their childcare, Sloe. Trust Sloe."

The Old Woman's eyes clouded over. She let her hand slip from Laura's. "But take fear of the girl called Flight. She's the one who'd steal Spellhorn from you. Take care..."

Her eyelids fluttered shut again. She shuffled round under her furs, wanting to sleep, but there were more things that Laura needed to know.

"Old Woman, why do you hate Flight? And why does she hate me?"

The Old Woman puffed out her lips in thought. Then she shrugged her bony shoulders. "It's the battlebite of the Mighty Highs, that's what. In her mind-hole Flight thinks you've stole her right place."

"But I have," Laura said. "If she's the oldest girlchild, she should be your leader."

The Old Woman shook her head. "Not without her mystery. Longtime past Flight could have been our Mighty High. She had the mystery, the special thing that gave her power to be our Mighty High, that's sure. But she used it wrong and then she lost it. She shut her eyes to it. It's all drained away. Like mine… like mine."

She squeezed Laura's arm.

"But you have the mystery, Girlchild. It's in your mind's eye. You can see where there's darkness. You have midnight eyes, like mine. That's why I pass to you the Mighty High. Safekeep the Wild Ones! Give me your forever word."

"I will," Laura said. Her throat was as dry as paper. "I promise."

The Old Woman nodded, and sank back on to her leafbed.

"Now. Don't be heartshaken. I'm heart weary, just an Old Bones now, know that. I'm wanting my forever sleep, that's all. Fetch Sideman to me."

She snuggled into her fur cover, the white hair tangled across her face, her breath snorting in light sleep. Laura took a last look at her.

"Goodbye, Old Woman," she whispered.

Then she crawled out of the tent and ran to find Sideman.

It was night-time, and bitterly cold. Mrs Brook went out into the garden, where Sam stood every night, watching out for Laura.

"Sam, there's no point," she told him gently. "Come back into the house, where it's warm. You won't find her here."

"We might, Mrs Brook. She might be trying to find her way."

"Come on in, Sam."

"Please, Mrs Brook. Can't I take Queenie with me and search for her?"

"There's no hope. We won't find Laura now."

She turned away from Sam, too upset to say more. In the kitchen, Queenie whimpered as if she'd recognised the sound of Laura's name.

★　★　★

"Sideman!" Laura shouted. "Sideman. The Old Woman wants to say goodbye to you."

The old Wildman had been lying wide-eyed by the fire. When Laura called him he heaved himself up with a grunt and shuffled to the tent, saying nothing, his head bent, his long arms dangling by his sides. Spellhorn trotted over to Laura and whinnied softly to her.

"We'll wait here, shall we?" Laura said.

She settled herself on the soft grass and Spellhorn knelt down next to her. Above their heads the wind whistled round the branches of the trees where the warrior-worrier sat with drooping wings. Small groups of Wild Ones began to rouse themselves and creep to the tent. They rubbed ash from the dead fires on to their arms and legs and faces, so they looked dusty and ghostly in the half light. They began a low moaning chant. Someone was playing a reed pipe, very softly, a watery trickling sound that was gentle and soothing. Laura knew that it was a sleeping song for the Old Woman, and that there was nothing to be afraid of. She closed her eyes and pillowed her head on Spellhorn's soft warm side, and slept.

And in the swirling dark of her mind's eye she saw four shapes running up the slope of a dipdown. Far below them the men shelters glowed with orange eyes. The two tall shapes cupped their hands over their mouths and called something, a name, a strange makesmile name, over and over again. Another shape ran to join them, smaller, with a lighter voice. And running round them was an earth beast on all fours. It ran with its head almost touching the ground, as if it was trying to catch noseful of something. Then it scampered off towards the shadowness of the trees, and the other shapes caught eye-sight, and quick ran after it.

Laura woke up suddenly. Spellhorn was standing next to her, his head up high. He was bellowing. It was broad daylight. The sky was green. The huge warrior-worrier flapped its rag wings above her. The voices of the Wild Ones shrieked round her like the wind. Sideman halted them all.

"The Old Woman wanders alone," he told them.

Then the Wild One voices came and went like the waves of the sea, rolling and rising, dark and soft:

> The Old Woman wanders alone
> Loose is the littering of leaves in the late of the year
> The hail is harsh when the ice will bind our hearts
> Frost fringes owl feathers, ravens freeze in flight
> The wind is a knife that whittles the worry of life
> But sweet is the song of the sun on the swan-road home
> Where the Old Woman wanders alone...

Laura sat up, rubbing her eyes. Water was kneeling by her.

"Girlchild, I've come to ask you to give help hand with the flower gathering," she said.

"What's happened?" asked Laura. "Has the Old Woman died?"

Water nodded. "All over now. She's sleeping her last forever sleep. Soon we'll have the goodbye-say to her, down by the sea. Wayfinder and Sloe have gone with the men to make a boat. She'll take her last sea journey in it. Come with the Wild Women."

Wild Women and Girls followed Laura as she went with Water. They looked at her shyly, reaching out their hands to touch her or to stroke her hair, patting her cheeks. Water clucked at them to keep back. They stopped in a clearing that was full of flowers and their perfumes, and knelt by them.

"Earth flowers are like earth beasts," Water told Laura. "They make the Wild Ones heartglad. And when we pluck them, we take only what we need, no more. While the girls pluck flowers, the Wild Women will weave them into two cloaks. One for the Old Woman, for the goodbye-say. And one for you. This night come moon-up, Girlchild, you'll wear this cloak at the welcome to the Mighty High."

The Wild Girls and Women bent to their work, plucking the flowers quickly and sorting them out into colours and shades for the two cloaks. Laura knew that two people were watching her, and she looked up at last to catch eyesight of them. One was Sloe. He had tied a broad leaf round his head to keep his long hair back and to stop the sweat trickling down into his eyes. He'd been with the Wildmen, hacking away at an old tree trunk to hollow it out, and still carried his stone axe with its finely chiselled blade. When Laura caught his eye he held his fist up in greeting to her, and went back to his work.

And the other was Flight. She was crouched on all fours in the long grass, her eyes bright as a watching bird's.

"Wordspeak," she hissed at Laura. "Right soon."

The sun blazed through the high trees, sharp as needle-points. And from all their high places in the far hills of the Wilderness the warrior-worriers came down, shaking their huge ragged tatters of wings, screeching their shrill cries of sadness: sadness and danger to the Wild Ones.

Chapter Fourteen

LAMENT FOR OLD BONES

FLIGHT DARTED AWAY from the Wild Women into an overhang of trailing leaves. After a bit Laura followed her, loping along on all fours because it was easier that way. She was curious to know why Flight wanted her, but she was afraid, too.

"The Old Woman said I should no time have wordspeak with you, Flight," she said.

Flight smiled, cocking her head to one side. "But

the Old Woman is dead! Know that. Now, take earful of this, Girlchild. Do you still have longings for your manfolk land?"

Laura searched inside herself. Here in the Wilderness she felt perfectly happy, everything was as it should be. And yet she had a tiny ache that she had no name for. "I don't know," she said. "My rememberings make me sad, that's all."

"I have a fancy plan for you in the think-hole of my mind," said Flight, tapping her head. "Come darkfall at the goodbye-say, if you're fearless, you could take your chance for home. Trust me, and think on!"

She scampered away. Spellhorn nosed his head through the overhang, whinnying softly, and Laura crawled out to him. She put her arms round his neck.

"Spellhorn, I can't go, can I?" she whispered. "I promised the Old Woman. And besides I want to stay forever time with you. Would you go with me to the manfolk land?"

Spellhorn snorted and tossed back his head.

"Never come to my flowerden, or leave your scent for me to smell?"

He pawed the earth.

"Would you come to the secret hiding-place of my mind's eye?"

He drew away from her and turned, stamping the ground, kicking his legs as she tried to get near him again, then galloped away. She ran out and watched him, his broad muscles flexing, his long legs leaping, his proud head held high. He pounded across the full length of the shoreline, sending up sand like smoke; the fastest of the earth beasts, the strongest, and the most beautiful.

"How could I leave him?" she thought. "He's all mine now."

From far away, like a sound in a dream, came a distant howl, then another. It came from the other side of the sea. It came from a memory. The Wild Ones heard it and stopped their work; holding their heads back, listening. The warrior-worriers heard it and rose up from their roosts, spreading out the rags of their wings like battle banners, circling the sky without sound. The howl came again, shivering down into a low whine. Wayfinder and Sideman clambered up Farlook Hill.

"Have you a memory of that sound?" asked Wayfinder.

The old Wild Man growled. "It's an earth beast of the menfolk. If it leads menfolk to our Wilderness then we're alltime lost. Our Wild One life would go forever, know that."

They gazed up at the circling warrior-worriers.

"They'll shred the earth beast if he comes close enough!" Wayfinder laughed.

Sideman cuffed him with his fist and crawled away down the stone. But Wayfinder stood, a puzzled trouble in his heart, gazing across the sun-striped sea. He remembered standing above the dipdown that led down to the manfolk shelters, long ago, far away, when the Wild Ones had been searching for Spellhorn. He remembered the sadness he had felt then, and how it had puzzled his heart. One day, perhaps, come time, Wild Ones and menfolk would be the same. "But not yet time," he said. He knuckled together his clenched fists. "Not yet time."

And Laura heard the howl. Deep inside her she felt her memory flickering. It was a home sound.

By the time dusk came the cloaks were ready. Laura had helped to weave the flowers into the Old Woman's cloak. It had been dipped in damson dyes and spread out on a tree to dry. It fluttered there, dark as night, and it smelt of rich fruits.

Water came to her with the other cloak, holding it out for her to see.

"Here, Girlchild," she smiled. "Here's your sunrise cloak, silksoft and petalsweet. All dawn colours."

The cloak looked as delicate as the reflection of flowers on water, as if to touch it would break up its colours. She held out her arms and Water slipped it across her shoulders. It was cool and fragrant. She laughed, swirling round so the cloak swayed and rippled over her. The Wild Women clustered round, grinning and clucking their approval. They had painted their faces by daubing coloured stripes on their cheekbones.

As light faded things seemed to happen very quickly. The men and boys came down from the spindle woods, carrying the trunk they'd hollowed for a boat. The prow was carved in the shape of a unicorn's head and painted white. Spellhorn was brought to Laura and she was helped on to his back.

"Be heartstrong, child of the Wild Ones," Water whispered. She arranged the cloak so it draped over Spellhorn's sides. Laura saw her spreading the damson cloak over the boat, and knew that the Old Woman was inside it, calm in her long, last sleep.

Then young Wild Men began to beat the drum slowly, and Sideman stepped forward to lead the goodbye-sayers to the sea. The boat bearers followed him, bent-backed under their burden, and Laura and Spellhorn followed them. Behind them came all the Wild Ones, echoing Spellhorn's chant or making up songs of their own as they thought of them; and then came the horses, clopping in their own slow pace, with leaves and dark flowers twisted into their manes.

The procession stopped at the water's edge. The boat was lowered on to the sand, waves lapping its hull.

Sideman turned to face everyone, and one by one the voices of the Wild Ones rose up to follow his:

"I, Sideman,"

"And I, Wayfinder,"

"I, Water,"

"And I, Sloe,"

"Horseman, Flamefinder, Grubwoman, Song Girl, Flight,"

"Grass, Ash, Fastfoot, Fern."

"And all the Wild Ones, weeping in their hearts…"

"… come to the silk sea for the goodbye-say."

The boat bearers bent again and pushed against the log, and with a grating sigh it hushed down into the waves. The Wild Ones began to moan low in their throats.

Laura felt something tugging at her cloak. It was Flight.

"Girlchild, now's the chance—" Flight began earnestly.

"Flight, aren't you heartsad?"

"Fill your eyes with weep rain, but fill your ears with my wise words. The feeling in my heart is that the Wild Ones should never go to the manfolk land again. We are no longer heartglad there, or safe. And my other feeling is that you will never be heartglad in the Wilderness. Our time is not your time. Our Wild One ways aren't yours."

Laura turned away, sad. In her thoughts she heard the whimperings of a strange beast. Beneath her Spellhorn pawed the sand, tossing up his head. She could hear the great watch birds treading the sky with their tattered wings, waiting to strike down strangers.

"Give me your flower cloak," urged Flight.

"Why?" Laura clutched it round herself as if a sudden cold wind had chilled her.

"Because it belongs to the Wilderness. And you'll make your way more safekeep without it."

Spellhorn whinnied.

"I can't. I can't go, Flight."

The chanting voices rose. Flight grasped Laura's hand, trying to pull her down. "When the boat begins to flame, all the eyes of the Wild Ones will be turned that way. No one will catch eyesight of you. Head for home!"

Laura watched the group of Wild Ones in the half-light, as they gathered up their sharpened arrows to dip in Flamefinder's fire.

"But what about them?" she said. "What will they do without a Mighty High?"

"I'll be their Mighty High!" Flight clapped her hands and danced round Laura. "I'm the one. I know it. Give me the flower cloak and they'll think I'm you, and speak the welcome words to me."

Laura shook her head.

"They will!" insisted Flight. "And when you've gone they'll be heartglad to have me in your place."

She tried to ease the cloak off Laura's shoulders.

Laura clutched at it. "Please leave me alone, Flight. Please go."

Spellhorn stamped, scudding up sand into Flight's face, but still the Wild Girl clung on.

A flame burst near the water's edge. Sideman dipped his arrow into it and turned round to face the Wild Ones again. He looked ghostly in the yellow light; he had painted white rings round his eyes, so they looked enormous and sorrowing. He stretched the beast gut that was the string of his bow.

"Send the flaming arrows streaking like firebirds across the foam!" he shouted.

"When they hit home, let the boat burn down to bone ash," said Flamefinder.

"May she forever float on the whalewaves of the sea!" said Wayfinder.

"Now!" said Sideman. "Let fly!"

Streaks of fire hissed across the dark sky and hit the bark of the Old Woman's floating tree. The white unicorn prow-head gleamed.

All the Wild Ones clustered down to the water's edge watching the boat take fire. Laura and Flight watched them from their shadow bay.

"If you don't take this now time it will never come again," whispered Flight.

Still Laura couldn't move. There were so many things she wanted to know.

"Flight. Please tell me this. Why did the Old Woman hate you?"

Flight looked down. "I am the only girlchild in her family. I had her gift of Mighty High, her mystery. And I lost it, long ago."

"How?" Then Laura remembered something that Sloe had told her, the night of the battlebite. "Flight, were you one the moonbats stole away?"

Flight nodded. "They lifted me up when I was a crawling child and hid me in their cave, longtime, longtime. Spellhorn nearly lost his life to search for me. But when he found me, my Mighty High had gone."

Laura considered this. Perhaps she'd been wrong about Flight after all.

"Poor Flight! And you have no rememberings of it?"

"Maybe it's curled up in the deep hiding-places of my mind-hole, but I can't find it there. And the Old Woman told me my good mystery is turned to bad, and I'm no way fit to be the Mighty High of the Wild Ones. But I want! I want!"

The burning boat flared on the black-green water. Laura saw Sloe glancing round, searching for her. She saw Wayfinder and Water standing with their arms across each other's backs for comfort. She belonged to them now.

And how would the Wild Ones manage without their Mighty High?

"I can't," she said. "I gave my promise word to Old Bones. I can't let you take my place without your mystery. You'd be useless to the Wild Ones, know that. Menfolk would come and take your Wilderness away, be sure."

Flight moaned. She swayed backwards and forwards, digging her knuckles into her eyes.

"If only I could see your mystery," said Laura. She slipped down off Spellhorn's back. She closed her eyes, letting the memory of the firelight flicker away, losing the colour of the green-black sea with its red glow. She walked along the sea edge, looking into her darkness, concentrating on the picture in her mind's eye. Foam licked round her feet. Shades and shapes began to swim about in her mind, slowly, as if they were wading through deep mud. And gradually a picture of Flight began to take shape. It made Laura grow cold with trickles of fear, because she knew she'd found Flight's mystery, and that it was a terrible thing.

"I can see you!" she gasped.

"But you have shut eyes," whispered Flight, scared. "Open your eyecovers, Girlchild!"

But Laura shook her head. The picture of Flight was very clear in her mind now. If she opened her eyes or gave a word-picture of it she knew it would fade away, perhaps for ever. Frightened though she was, she had to explore it until she knew the worst of it.

In the swirls of her mind's eye she saw a dark cave. Moonbats hung in it, opening out their leathery wings. On the damp floor of the cave a small girl sat: the child Flight. The child was not afraid, she was laughing. One of the moonbats swooped down and the Flightchild clambered on to its back. It rose up slowly and she spurred him on and out of the cave with kicks and shouts. The other moonbats swarmed out of the cave after them. They swirled out into the sky and headed through the night to the black trees of the Bad Woods. As they hovered, they lit up the earth with the light of their wings. A pale creature stood alone under the trees. As they plunged nearer to it the Flightchild on the moonbat leader's back shrieked with joy. "*Kill him!*" she shouted. "*Kill the unicorn!*"

Laura opened her eyes and stared at Flight. "I don't believe you were stolen by the moonbats, Flight. You wanted to be with them!"

Flight edged away from her. Her eyes were gleaming with laughing hate. "They're my flightfriends now," she hissed. "All badheart!"

"You could have flown with the warrior-worriers, the Wilderness birds. That was your mystery!" Laura said slowly. It was almost as if the Old Woman's voice was in her head now, whispering secret things. "And you chose to be with the moonbats instead. I know you now, Flight. If you took my place, you'd lead the Wild Ones to their death."

Chapter Fifteen

THE BATTLE OF THE MIGHTY HIGHS

THE FLAME WAS like a candleglow on the water, and the Wild Ones watched in silence as it floated away from them.

At last Sideman said in his gruff voice, "Forever lost in sleep is the old Mighty High. Now time for the welcome-say to the new."

"Where is the girlchild?" asked Wayfinder. "Spellhorn stands alone."

Sloe had seen Laura go with Flight. He'd watched her flower cloak drifting down to the far end of the shore, and the sight of that had made him anxious.

"Let me go seekfind her at the far-off shore," he said. As he ran he heard the soft scuff of hooves on the sand, and knew that Spellhorn was following him. Soon the unicorn overtook him.

Flight had led Laura till they were both standing knee-deep in the water. Warrior-worriers swooped soundlessly over their heads, sensing a danger to the Wild Ones. Their beaks were open, their eyes sharp-bright. Spellhorn splashed into the sea. Laura felt her throat tighten at the sound, and at the touch of his silky hair on her cheek.

"Girlchild..." called Sloe.

"I'm ready, Sloe," she said.

She ran back to him. He slapped the palm of his hand across his forehead to show he'd been worried about her. She laughed and swung up on to Spellhorn's back and the unicorn held his head high and bucked up his back legs. Then he galloped at full speed across the sand. Sloe ran behind, shouting at Laura to wait for him. Flight dragged the sand with her feet, head down.

"Well come the Mighty High!" shouted Wayfinder as soon as he saw Laura.

"Well come!" the Wild Ones called. "Well come!"

They surrounded her in a dancing throng, leading her

back with them away from their sad thoughts of grief for the Old Woman, back to the huge fires that Flamefinder had built for them near the word circle. The singing and celebrating lasted through the night and well into the next day. Laura fell asleep long before all the welcome-sayings were done and it didn't matter; the Wild Ones went on saying them till one by one they dropped off too, just where they were sitting. They rolled over with their reed pipes still clutched in their hands, with their fingers stretched to pluck the strings of their gut harps. The dancers sank to their knees in mid dance, and the singers' voices wound down into snores. The sky turned black and bright again before any of them woke up, and some still snored when the next moon came up.

Laura was one of the last of all to wake. She went down to the river rush to wash herself. Her legs were aching with all the dancing she'd been doing, and her throat was sore with singing. She lay back in the water, enjoying its sparkle. Sideman splashed over to join her and, grunting with the effort, squatted down beside her.

"Right good happytime, that was," Laura said.

"The Wild Ones need a wordspeak at day-down," he told her. "There's worryings around."

"Are there?" Laura asked. "What about?"

"Flight," he muttered. From where they squatted they could see Flight moving about among the Wild Ones.

They could hear the ring of argument in their voices, though they couldn't hear any of the words. When the Wild Girl saw that they were watching her she crouched down on all fours and glared at them.

"She has heart-hate of me," said Laura. "And alltime will. She calls herself Mighty High."

Sideman snorted. "Two Mighty Highs! There's no good in that. Two moons would tear the sea in half. Two suns would burn the earth away. This will bring woe to the Wilderness, know that!"

He crawled away, gulping up water and spitting it out to the side as he went. Laura watched him. Did he still think she was an intruder? Would he rather have Flight after all? But she had no way of showing him what she'd seen in her mind's eye. She swam further up the river, to where it widened out and deepened into lagoons. Sloe and Fern were diving off high rocks. She scrambled up to join them, and soon she was laughing with them and plunging again and again into bluey-green water. It was so clear that when she stood on the top of the diving-rock she could see the reflection of herself poised to dive, with her hair long and loose around her. As she dived it spread out behind her like wings.

"Flight!" Sloe called out, seeing the Wild Girl watching them. "Do this! Then you'd proper fly!" Flight turned her back on him.

At day-down, the Wild Ones gathered from the sea's edge and from the spindle woods and streams. They came, in muttering groups of twos and threes, to take their places round the speaking circle. By the time Laura arrived with Sloe and Fern, Flight was already there. Sideman motioned to everyone to squat down and he hunkered down on his haunches in the middle of them. There was to be no singing this time, Laura could see that. Sloe went to sit among the other Wild Boys and Water called him over to her. She whispered something to him. He hid his face behind his hands and shook his head. Water pulled his hands away and, laughing, nodded to him. This time Sloe loped over to Laura, cheeks bulging, and squatted down at her side.

"There might be fisty fights. I'll be the punchboy," he told her.

"You will not," Laura said. "There'll be no fisty fights while I'm Mighty High. Anyway, I can do my own punching."

She pushed her fists into his knees and he fell back, feet paddling into the air. Sideman snorted and came to sit at Laura's other side. Sloe swung himself back up and rubbed his knees. The Wild Ones fell silent. Laura realised that they were all watching her, waiting for her to speak. She began nervously.

"My words to you are full of welcome smiles, as this is

the first wordspeak of your new Mighty High." The Wild Ones nudged each other, chuckling across at her. Water clapped her palms silently together. Laura glanced at Sideman, not knowing whether she was expected to say anything else. He sat with his knees up and his elbows resting on them, his chin cupped in his hands, rumbling in the back of his throat. He was watching Flight, who sat slightly out of the word circle, her head back and her eyes closed, as if she was asleep or bored. So there was more to say.

"But there are worryings in our Wilderness," Laura went on. The Wild Ones grunted. "While I am Mighty High I want all minds to be together, all in one peace." Again there were mutterings and head scratchings.

"If you have no heart for me to be your Mighty High, say so and have done."

The Wild Ones looked down. Some of them began to scratch on the earth with their toenails, drawing trees and birds, or to plait their long hair and beards. They all avoided each other's eyes.

"Say now," Laura went on, feeling stronger. "This is the last speak about this thing."

"I say so!" hissed Flight.

The Wild Ones stopped fidgeting. Laura stood up slowly and Flight sprang to her feet. She danced round Laura, all leap and lightfeet, baffling her. Her hair swung out like loose and shaggy feathers. She lashed out with her legs and her arms, snapped her fingers, click-clicked with her tongue, spat and laughed. She was quick fire, and Laura, spinning round to keep her in sight, felt herself growing weak with dizziness. Sloe jumped up next to Laura and buckled up his fists to fight.

"You sit down," she told him. He sank back, disappointed, sticking out a leg now and then to try to trip Flight up. "Chuck her in worm spit," he advised.

"What cure is there for this, Flight?" Laura asked.

The Wild Girl whipped out at her with her hair and her limbs. Clucking and sighing behind their hands, the Wild Ones shuffled back, and Laura stood cold in the middle of Flight's circle of fury. "I must stay calm," she told herself. "I can't match her wildness, no chance. But one of us has to be the strong one. It must be me."

She heard a whinnying from the edge of the spindle woods. Spellhorn was watching her, then. That gave her strength.

"If you won't have me as your Mighty High, then I won't let you live among the Wild Ones," Laura said.

Flight stopped her frenzied dance.

"This is my Mighty High word to you," Laura went on, so softly that the listeners had to strain their ears to hear what she was saying to Flight. "Live out of sight of us, all days."

The Wild Ones jumped to their feet. Some of them were cheering, some protesting. They clamoured round her.

"Those who make choice of Flight for their Mighty High go with her." Laura was shaking, but she managed to keep her voice low and steady. "That's the ending of my wordspeak."

She walked away from the babble of voices that rose up round her and perched on a low rock near the fires that Flamefinder had made. She felt as if she was cold right inside her bones.

Flight, too, ran away from the group and then paused with her arms spread out and one leg trailing behind her, like a bird stopped in mid-air. Some of the younger Wild Ones began to run after her. Their parents called them back and, one by one, they came. Laura sat with her back to them all, gazing into the flames of the fire, not daring to look. She could hear the whisper of feet on sand as they edged across to her. For a long time Sideman stood staring at Flight. He sighed and shook his head many times. Then like an old dog when all its fight has gone, he turned and limped over to the fires. The last of all to move was Wayfinder. He stood with his fists clenched and his eyes closed.

"Come," coaxed Water.

"Never have the Wild Ones been split up, no time," he sighed. "There's deep heart heaviness in this."

But at last he came. The word circle where they'd all sat was silent and empty. No one spoke or moved now. The only thing to be heard was the crackling of the fire flames. Then there came a terrible wailing. Flight ran through the deep shadows of the spindle trees and into the high tree places and past them, into the dark wild heart of the Wilderness. Long after she'd gone, and long after the Wild Ones had found their skin shelters and curled themselves up wearily and sadly for the night, the wailing was heard, and it was like the sound of a beast in pain.

Chapter Sixteen

THE COMING OF MENFOLK

THE SUN AND moon came and went many times, and
Flight wasn't seen again in the Wilderness. Laura often
wondered what had happened to her. Sometimes she felt
that she would have liked to have gone deep into the
Wilderness in search of her, but she knew that would be
wrong. She was the Mighty High, and she had made the
decision about banishing Flight. That must be the end of
it. Still she felt sad. Sloe came across her one day sitting

by herself. She pretended to be concentrating on weaving flowers together to drape across the opening of her skin tent, but really her mind was on Flight, worrying for her. He squatted near her, watching her, puzzled by her quiet mood. He slapped his forehead, and she smiled at him.

"Are you still heartglad here?" he asked her.

"Of course I am," she said. "I was just looking at all these flower lights, and thinking how they make me happysad."

He pulled a face. "Happysad? Show me the number one happy flower then."

She pointed to a blue one with wide petals. "That's a makepeace colour. And all the leaves make me feel wet grass calm."

Sloe gathered some red flowers and danced round with them. "These ones give me jump joy," he laughed. "But there's danger in them too."

"And this one?" He took the pale lilac-grey one she handed him. "Does this give you crying quiet?"

He nodded, and pointed to a spray of yellow. "That colour's for heart gladness. You should keep these in your hair."

"And these are for you, Sloe." Laura draped some tiny white flowers round his shoulders. "These make me feel all hush. You should wear them some time, then we'd have shush in the Wilderness!"

He sat down by her. "And what does this one do?" He picked a large purple flower with deep velvety petals and a dark, open mouth. "This one jags me, this light."

"Does it?" She took it from him. "It's dream deep, I think."

"Last sleep dream, then," he shuddered. "With hurt."

He scooped up the flowers they'd picked and showered them over her, so their petals fluttered into her eyes and her mouth.

"There's dizzyings now for you!" he laughed. "Flower-light rain."

He ran off, shouting to Fastfoot to help him run messages round the Wilderness. Laura lay back among the petals, breathing in the scent that was the colour of yellow to her. She looked up at the fronds and leaf fingers, the lovely shapes of them. It was as she'd wanted it to be now, all in one peace. There were no quarrellings.

Yet the warrior-worriers had stayed. She could see them crouched in the branches above her head. At night, while the Wild Ones slept under the huge and brilliant stars, Laura could hear the birds frilling out their feathers and cackling softly to each other. Why didn't they go back to their mountain roosts? What were they waiting for?

And one day, Sloe brought them heartstop news. Day by day the Wild Ones all had to take a turn at eye spy from Farlook Hill. He'd been on watch all day. He came stumbling off the hill at day-down, waving his arms and shouting, dropping down on all fours and tumbling over himself in his anxiety. Wayfinder ran to meet him.

"Sloe! Take air gulps!" he told him.

Sloe gasped for breath while the Wild Ones crowded round him.

"Now tell everything," said Wayfinder.

"Menfolk!" panted Sloe.

"Menfolk?" The Wild Ones looked round at each other in disbelief.

Sloe nodded. "Menfolk on big logs. Bird boats on the worm sea…"

"Menfolk must never, never come to the Wilderness," said Sideman. "Never no time."

"But they are coming! There's big tree birds on the water, with menfolk riding them…"

The Wild Ones looked at Laura for guidance. She was trembling.

"What will happen will happen," she said at last. "If menfolk have found a way to the Wilderness, we can't stop them."

"I say this is no time right for menfolk and Wild Ones to come close," said Wayfinder, shaking his head. "Our ways are not their ways."

"We'll give them welcome-songs," suggested Water.

"They'll see it's our happy place and they'll leave us to our peace days."

"They'll snatch it!" Sideman growled. "They'll call it manfolk land, all theirs!"

"Take sharp sticks and lobbing stones," suggested Sloe. "Throng on the sea edge and chuck things at them!"

"I'll fling fire!" said Flamefinder.

"Right good!" the Wild Ones shouted. They hurried off to find weapons.

"No!" shouted Laura. "That's not good. Menfolk won't come to harm us."

"Then what for have they come?" Sideman demanded.

Laura faltered. "Perhaps… perhaps for looksee," she suggested. She looked round at the Wild Ones. "But I'm the Mighty High, and this is my wordspeak. No sharp sticks. No fling stones. No fire. Let them meet us as we are, all gentlekind."

Reluctantly the Wild Ones did as they were told. They dropped their hunting spears and the small sharp stones they were cradling in their palms. They followed Laura and Sideman and Sloe to Farlook Hill, and, in silence, gathered on its slopes. They stood with their arms round each other; a little excited, a little scared.

The sea was a misty swirl of silver grey. Shapes lurked and fluttered just out of sight. There seemed to be a billowing of wings. Not a sound came from the drifting mist. The Wild Ones peered out at them, rubbing their eyes. All the Wilderness colours had drained away, and its sky had grown dark as night. Laura put her hands round her eyes, tunnelling what light there was. Was there something there? Strange that there was no sound, no slap of waves or shout, no lights or flickerings, only grey shapes in a grey mist, looming.

She crept down past the silent Wild Ones to the very edge of the shore. If there were menfolk coming, she should be the first to greet them.

Suddenly, the sky above the mist seemed to break up into hundreds of dark pieces, like a showering of black splinters. As Laura watched, the splinters seemed to grow and take form; they were winged. They came steadily towards the Wilderness, and as the last pale light of day faded they opened up brilliant flashes. Now the leathery flap of the wings was quite distinct.

"Moonbats!" breathed Laura.

Their glow made a searchlight over the sea, and picked out the white wing-shapes of ships' sails. The moonbats were guiding them in. The leader broke away from the rest and swooped towards Laura, lighting her up in a white blaze. Flight was riding it. She clung to it with her arms round its neck and her legs tucked to its wings, screaming with laughter.

"Go back, Flight!" Laura called.

Flight turned round on her moonbat's back, and screeched out to the silent floating ships: "Take the girlchild! Here she is! Take her!"

Chapter Seventeen

THE WILDERNESS IN DANGER

FLIGHT SWERVED BACK towards Laura. She leaned down
and reached out to grab her, trying to pull her further
into the sea.

"They've come for you, Girlchild!"

Laura started to plunge away from her, still not
understanding what was happening.

"Now do you pass to me your Mighty High?" Flight
demanded. The moonbat lunged again. Laura's eyes were

scorched and scalded with its brightness. She crouched down, covering her face with her hands.

"No, Flight. No time."

Flight swung up and away from her and skimmed back towards the ghostly ships.

"Take the Wild Ones!" she shouted. "All yours!"

She swooped again, and the air roared round her. From the grey ghost ships came a boom like a mountain crack, then another and another, echo booms, booms and cracks, shudders of thunder and lightning strike, ocean voices.

The Wild Ones, huddled on the slopes of Farlook Hill, screamed and tumbled for shelter. Some of them fell in last sleep, like toppled trees. Laura stood knee deep in the water. The mist was white smoke now, in her eyes and over her skin, in her hair and in the holes of her nose and her mouth and her ears.

"Spellhorn!" she shouted. "Save us!"

The unicorn reared up from his sleeping-place. He bellowed to the waiting warrior-worriers, who had gathered round him to protect him from the menfolk. In answer, they howled and opened up their wings. They streamed out above and behind him in a long beating line as he plunged down to the sea edge; like a flight of horses they turned the air with their speed, and the scream of their wings was like the scrape of knives on stone.

Spellhorn plunged into the sea. Laura clung to him. The birds whistled past into the swirling streams of battle smoke to gash the moonbats' wings with their beaks, to shred the sails of the shadow ships, to beat around the heads of the warring menfolk, to make the ghost ships turn, and turn, and turn.

The moonbat leader dived down towards Laura, trying to drive her off Spellhorn's back into the sea. Flight leaned down and tried to kick her off, lashing out with her arms and legs.

"Flight, Flight!" Laura shouted, and her voice was hardly heard above the hollerings of battle. "Come back to the Wild Ones! Be one of us! You mustn't be our enemy. You'll destroy the Wilderness!"

Flight laughed. "I'll no time come back to you, Girlchild! I can be Mighty High of menfolk now. They'll follow me, all greedy hearts. We'll have your Spellhorn and your Wilderness, know that!"

"Then strike her, Spellhorn!" shouted Laura.

She clung on to him as he tipped slowly backwards, until he was upright on his hind legs. As the moonbat swooped again, he stabbed it through. Flight flung out her arms and screamed. Spellhorn tossed his head with the great moonbat spiked on his horn. The moonbat ripped itself free, its wings in shreds. Flight tumbled down into the sucking waves and was washed away.

Wild Ones, on eye-spy turn on Farlook Hill, spied her every day-down after that, a dark, flightless bird tossing about on the sea, lifting up its wings to fly and sinking down again, marooned for ever on the waters between manfolk land and Wilderness.

But now the sea was quiet. Spellhorn carried Laura back to the sleeping-place, and one by one the Wild Ones crawled back to join her. They were whimpering to themselves. All night they huddled together, licking each other's wounds. All was in darkness. Their fires had burnt down. Flamefinder was dead. In the darkness they called out their names to each other.

Wayfinder. Water. Sloe. Horseman. Grubwoman. Fastfoot. Woodfetch. Rain… Their voices were weak and afraid… Healhands… Star… Stoneshift… Girlchild… the names fluttered quietly like candles… Small One… Berrygather… Tree…

Yet there were many names missing. Sideman's name wasn't there. So he had found his last forever sleep. And there were more whose names were never heard again. Grass, with her dancing. And Song Girl. Sweet Fern. Ash…

Day came with all its blaze of brilliance. The mists had cleared away and the sea was sparkling again. It was nearly impossible to believe that the terrible thing had really happened. But it was all over. The Wild Ones were calm in their grieving. They set about gathering flowers and hollowing out logs for the goodbye-say for their dead. Healhands searched out herbs and plants and Laura and Water helped her to rub them into the wounds of the injured Wild Ones. The warrior-worriers had flown back to their mountain homes. The birds of the Wilderness set up their clear piping.

Laura sat with the older girls helping to weave the flower cloaks. There must never be a time like this for the Wild Ones again, she thought. She must do something to make sure it never happened again.

"The feeling in my heart is this," she told Water. "I must give something to menfolk, to make sure they leave the Wilderness alone for ever."

"You?" Water smiled sadly. "What could you give to menfolk, Girlchild?"

Chapter Eighteen

SPELLHORN GOES MISSING

NEXT DAY SPELLHORN went missing. Laura and Sloe searched for him round the Wilderness, but there was no sign of him. They came back to the word circle tired and worried, and all the younger Wild Ones were put into groups to help them search again. There was nothing, not even a hoofprint on the sand. Laura kept thinking she could hear the fluty sound of his whinnying, but when she looked round there was nothing there – the sound was in her head. At the end of the second day's searching she and Sloe scrambled up Farlook Hill. They could see the ice mountains sparkling in the crimson glow of the huge late sun; they could see the water on fire with it. A small dark bird hovered on the water far out, beating its wings to try to lift itself up, falling, lifting, falling.

But there was no sign of Spellhorn. Laura said she wanted to stay on the hill all night to watch out for him. She sat hunched up there when the sun slid down into the sea, and when the moon like a boat rocked up into the dark sky, and when the stars like eyes of ice stared down at her.

Sloe stayed with her for a long time. During the night he slipped away and came back with some food for her.

"Here," he said. "Sup some mush."

She shook her head. Soon Sloe fell asleep and at last, briefly, Laura did too; but only in snatches. She kept herself alert and listening out for Spellhorn all the time, and every slight sound of the creatures of the Wilderness moving along their prowl paths jerked her awake. When she did sleep she had strange, disturbing dreams of dark figures looming towards her out of a swirling mist. They reached out to her, and in her dream she reached out to them, stretching hand to hand, fingertips almost touching, before the figures slipped away back into the mist. She could hear midnight voices calling out a name that she didn't recognise.

Next morning she searched round the Wilderness again. The Wild Ones watched her, helpless. It was a makesad thing, they said. They slapped their foreheads and sniffed round for scent of him, mystified. At last Laura crept to her skin tent and lay there in darkness, staring up at the swaying hides. Water crawled in to see her with life sip for her to drink. She sat back, watching Laura quietly.

"Wild Ones have never known heartsad times like this," she said.

"It's my blame shame," said Laura. "I've done the Mighty High all wrong."

Water laughed and patted Laura's cheeks. "You're a right good Mighty High, Girlchild. Know that."

"Then where's my Spellhorn?"

Water shook her head and sighed. "Shuteye now. Let me do the sleeping–hum for you. He'll come."

As Water sang Laura felt herself beginning to drift away. Day seeped into night and back again and still she slept. Sloe watched anxiously by her side. He prodded her from time to time to try to wake her up, till at last Water made him go away and leave her alone. And during the next night Laura woke up. All the Wild Ones were snoring in gentle sleep. She lay with her eyes wide open and knew that Spellhorn had come back.

She crawled out of the skin tent. Spellhorn was a pale light in the darkness, watching her.

"Spellhorn!" As soon as she moved towards him he bounded lightly away. He disappeared into the spindle trees.

"Wait!"

She ran after him, laughing, following the moonflashes of his white flicking mane through the trees. He seemed to be leading her towards the rushdown. She could hear the tumble of its water gush. She came at last to where he was waiting by a cave mouth. She ran to him and hugged him, burying her face in the warmth of his neck. Her heart was thudding and her arms and legs were trembling. "Where did you go?" she asked. "Why did you leave me?"

He drew away from her slightly. She realised that they were standing outside the cave where she and Sloe had made pictures of their names together, ages past. Spellhorn blew softly on her cheeks and pawed the earth.

"What's in there, Spellhorn? Have you found something?" she asked.

He whinnied.

She drew back the trailing curtain of moss and fern that covered the cave mouth and peered in. It was too dark to see anything, yet she had a sense that something was in there, breathing.

"Who's there?" she asked.

Nothing.

She crawled into the cave and reached out, groping into the darkness. She touched skin. A hand.

"Who is it?"

"Who is it?" A voice came back, like hers; a girl's voice, shaking.

"I'm Girlchild," said Laura. "I'm the Mighty High of the Wild Ones."

"I'm Midnight."

"Midnight!" Laura sat back on her heels. Midnight. That was a something special name. There was a mystery in that, all right. There were faraway rememberings there, too. She heard Spellhorn moving quietly behind her.

"Come outside, Midnight," she said. "I want to see you."

She crawled backwards out of the cave and the Midnight girl followed her slowly. Already it was nearly day. As Laura stood up outside the cave she could see how awkwardly Midnight was groping, feeling her way into the light. She stood up cautiously. She didn't look at Laura or at Spellhorn but gazed in front of her.

"You're not a Wild One," said Laura. The girl had pale skin and soft hair. Her blue eyes were blank and had no expression in them. She still gazed ahead of her, not minding Laura's stares.

"How did you get here?" Laura asked.

Midnight smiled and reached out her hand to pat Spellhorn's back. "Same as you," she said. "Spellhorn brought me."

Laura felt herself grow cold. "Spellhorn?"

She looked away. There was mystery about Midnight, well sure. She was afraid to meet her, and yet heartglad too. She felt she'd known her alltime.

"Come and take eyeful of the Wilderness," she said.

Midnight held out her hand, and Laura took it in her own. She guided the girl through the tangle of roots and wild plants that clustered round her feet. When they came to the rushriver that Laura always splashed through, Midnight clung to her with both hands and edged her way across, sliding one foot slowly in front of the other.

Further along the bank they came to a pool. It was cut away from the river and had no rush in it. It was calm and quite clear.

"Stop for a dip slosh," Laura told Midnight. She realised how tired she felt after all her waiting and watching. She squatted down by the pool and Midnight knelt beside her. Laura bent forward so her head was over the water and she could see her reflection in its stillness. Midnight leaned forward too, and Laura gazed at her own pale face, the yellow hair dangling, the blue eyes. So.

It was just as she had thought, deep inside herself. She and Midnight were the same.

Spellhorn thrust his nose down into the pool to drink, and the image shattered.

Laura sat back on her heels again.

"Don't you have eyebright?" she asked.

Midnight shook her head.

"Don't you see earth colours, flower lights, and all?"

"No."

"Then there's no heart happiness for you in the Wilderness," said Laura. She closed her eyes and tried to clear the confused images swimming in her head. Something was tugging at her memory, the way the river tugs at a leaf caught between stones. There was a word that she needed. "This is not the right homeland for you." That was the word. Homeland. Home. The leaf floated free. Spellhorn nudged her as if he was trying to wake her up from a sleep, and she opened her eyes again.

"Somewhere there's a home place, Midnight, that's for you. Where you'll be right heartglad, alltime. We must go there."

Midnight didn't say anything. She stood up when Laura did and let herself be led away from the pool. Spellhorn plunged into it and rolled over, kicking his legs. He stood up and shook the water off his coat and then trotted after Laura and Midnight. Laura stopped just outside the sleeping-place of the Wild Ones. Some of them were awake already, full of stretches and snorts. She could see Fastfoot's mouth wide open in a yawn. Sloe was scratching himself. Wayfinder tickled Water to make her sit up and then cuffed her, fist to fist, and laughed. Grubwoman shuffled after Woodfetch, muttering to herself, to find the day's first bellyfill.

Laura couldn't bring herself to go to them. She felt weak with a strange sadness. Sloe yawned and turned round, seeing her there, and held up his fist in a say-hello sign. Slowly she raised her own fist up to him. Then he dropped down on to all fours and scampered after Woodfetch.

"Safekeep well!" Laura whispered. Her throat ached with tightness. The way to her old homeland would be long and difficult. She might never get there. And she might never get back to the Wilderness, she knew that. "I'll always think of you."

She turned round to Midnight. The girl's face was white and strained.

"Clamber up," Laura told her. She helped Midnight on to Spellhorn's back and then climbed up behind her, reaching round her to hold her tight with her arms and to hang on to Spellhorn's mane. She kicked him gently, turning his head away from the Wild Ones.

"You know the where-way," she told him. "Now dash."

Chapter Nineteen

OVER THE ICE MOUNTAINS

SPELLHORN CHOSE TO go over the ice mountains. His feet
skittered to the sides from time to time with the speed of his
striding, but he never lost his footing. His hooves chimed on
the ice, and the chimes rang from peak to peak, till it seemed
as if a team of unicorns were galloping there in full flight.
Laura loved the speed and the wash of cold air on her face,
and the feel of her hair loose and streaming behind her.
Midnight clung to Spellhorn, laughing with excitement.

When they came down from the mountains, the air was soft and gentle on them. They slept as they rode and woke up refreshed and happy. They had no idea how long the journey took, or where they were travelling through. Spellhorn knew the way.

Once he stopped. They were on the top of a hill, looking down into a valley. They could see a small village below them, with one main street of houses. A boy was riding up and down it on his bike. He stopped for a moment and stood with his legs straddled each side of it, looking up towards them. He shielded his eyes against the sun. Laura waved to him. Before the boy had time to turn his bike round and look again they were off and out of sight and he was left, excited and bewildered, not sure about what he seemed to have seen.

Spellhorn slowed down again when he came to some boulders on the edge of the hill. He wove his way slowly through them, and down on to a path that led through an open space. Soon they came to some trees, and then the path ended halfway down the hillside, at the gate of a house. It was the last house in the village. Spellhorn leapt over the gate and picked his way down some steps into a garden. Laura ducked as he made his way under the knobbly branches of an apple tree. He stopped in a small flower garden.

"This must be your homeland place," said Laura.

She slipped down from Spellhorn's back and held up her hand to help Midnight, and as she did so all the lights of her world went down.

In the black, the deep swim of darkness she felt out and found nothing. She stretched out her arms and turned slowly round. Nothing. She stood still, trying to steady down her breathing. Now she could smell the rich earth under her feet. She moved forward again and touched the rough knobbled bark of the apple tree. She heard a dog barking and the scrabble of his paws against a door, and the sound of the door being opened. A shape of warm and hairy wetness flung itself at her.

"Queenie!" she laughed. "Queenie!"

People shouted; their running feet squelched on the grass. Her father's chin scratched her cheek. Her mother put her arms round her and held her and held her.

Home.

Chapter Twenty

HOMELAND

IN THE FLOWERDEN the strong spicy smell of cinnamon mingled with the scent of flowers. A glimmer of white moved in the shadows. Midnight stroked Spellhorn's back.

"The Wild Ones are waiting for their Mighty High, right sure," she said. She dug her heels firmly into his sides. "Hurry me home to them."

Postscript

Spellhorn actually began life as a play for radio. I had a request from Janet Whitaker, then a producer for BBC Radio 4 Schools programmes, to write a drama series about a unicorn. I was very excited by the idea, because of all the fabulous beasts, the unicorn seems to be the one that people love the most. In fact, many people really believe in them, and report that they have seen them. There are even records of people hunting them for the magical properties of their horns, or alicorns, which are said to cure many ills and to have the power of turning poisoned water fresh and pure. It is also said that a unicorn will only willingly come to a young maiden. I felt sure I would be able to make use of all these ancient folk themes.

I had recently written a novel, *Tough Luck*, in close consultation with a class of teenagers from a school in Doncaster, and had loved the experience. I felt it would be wonderful to involve children again in this new project. Radio writing is still my favourite medium, because it gives both the writer and the listener much more scope to use their imagination than television does. It creates pictures in your mind. How interesting it would be, I thought, to involve children for whom *sound* has a particular quality, who don't know things by seeing them, but by hearing them, as well as by touching, tasting and smelling them. I contacted a school for the visually impaired in Sheffield, Tapton Mount School, and asked if it would be possible to talk to some children there. At this stage I had no idea what I was going to do with them, or what would develop. I had had very little contact with the blind, and I was a little anxious about meeting these children. I also wanted to give something positive back to them. Sharing writing ideas is always a lovely experience, and I wanted it to be as rich as possible for all of us.

It was easily arranged. Four children made up one whole class! Their teacher, Pat Darley, was very happy for me to meet them and talk to them about writing. I called in on a fairly regular basis and soon got to know Holly, David, Robert and Richard quite well. I soon realised that they were just like any other children I'd met: boisterous, lively and full of fun and mischief. There was one difference, though, and that was very marked. They had a wonderful ability to listen and to remember. When I read extracts out to them they remembered it almost word for word the next week. I found that when I wrote for them I could use words in an inventive way that they understood and enjoyed.

I soon had a sense of how they worked as a group and how I could draw them out individually. Their range of visual impairment and experience varied. Richard and Robert had been blind from birth. David had lost his sight in an accident two years previously. Holly had cataracts, but could read very large print with the help of a strong light.

The story of my play was to be about a fantastic beast, but I began by asking the children to write, on their Perkins Braille typewriters, stories or poems about any animals. I was surprised to hear their descriptions, because you would not have known from any of them that they weren't sighted children, as they wrote about colour, shape and movement. Soon I realised that what they were doing is what most children do, in that they were reproducing what they had read in stories and poems written by sighted people. They were giving me what they thought I wanted. But I wanted much more. I wanted to encourage them to write from their own experience, using their *other* senses. We spent many hours together, writing and reading to each other, listening to sounds and making up words for them, listening to each other on the tape recorder, talking about their experiences of going swimming and visiting farms, going to disco parties, coming home with me.

Gradually I began to work on the radio play, which was called *A Dream of Unicorns*, but at the same time I wrote the story as a novel. I wanted to share it with the children at every stage, reading it to them chapter by chapter as I wrote it. All four of the children wanted my central character to be a girl. I called her Laura because in a famous poem by Petrarch, Laura is the name of a character who is drawn along by a team of unicorns. But I decided that my central character, Laura, was going to be blind, like them.

We had many discussions about the story as it developed. We decided that the Wild Ones would speak a strange language of their own, and we all made up different languages and taught them to each other. I based mine, the one that the Wild Ones speak in the book, on the idea of Anglo-Saxon kennings or 'picture-words'. We made up songs and invented instruments for the Wild Ones to play.

Unicorns appear in the ancient stories of many different cultures, and the more I read about them the more I wanted to create a mystical, glorious place for Spellhorn's paradise, which I called the Wilderness. With their teacher, the children built a model of the Wilderness, and we thought how waterfalls and caves and rocks would be magical and mysterious, as they were to ancient civilisations. We talked about who the Wild Ones were, and whether they would have any enemies. Robert told me that the most frightening experience he had ever had was when he was taken to a place where there were laser lights, because the brightness hurt his eyes so much. That was what gave me the idea for the moonbats. We each wrote a 'battlebite' scene between Spellhorn and the hornless unicorns, and when the children told me that my battle was too tame I put much more action in it to please them! But we all agreed that the greatest enemy of the Wilderness would be Man himself.

I think *Spellhorn* is my most imaginative book, and it is certainly the one that gave me the most pleasure to write. The more I got to know the children, the more I was able to enter their world of darkness, and I think that it was Holly, David, Richard and Robert who gave me the courage to let my imagination go free.

BERLIE DOHERTY

July 2002